MYSTERY ONE™ SERIES

Caught by a Cat

Not a Childrens' Book

Acknowledgments

Many thanks to the people who gave me ideas and suggestions that are incorporated in this book.

Detective Mark Brizendine, of the Anderson (IN) Police Department, reviewed the MS and looked for procedural SNAFUs.

My sister, Theresa, added balance to the characters and proofread the MS.

Stan Mondala corrected my Yiddish and offered helpful ideas.

Debra Robinson uncomfortably but productively made me think about the ending.

Judy Otterson encouraged me to write this book.

Thanks to all those on Facebook who commented on the various cover proposals.

Some mention of gratitude must be made to my cats, Moochie and Scraggles, for giving me the initial idea of how a criminal's identification could be made.

And special thanks to Claudia Pfeiffer, who suffered through numerous pre-draft editions and ideas, and who cleaned up the text and kept me on message.

-ooo-

and it's tied up with rope. And maybe duct tape."

"Can you tell what it is?"

"I can tell it shouldn't be here. Do you want me to go get it?"

"No. Please wait there until the police arrive. Are you alone?"

"No, I'm with someone. Do you want to talk to him?"

"No, that's okay. Can you have him go up the bank, to the Burger King parking lot, to help the police find you? Are you safe there by yourself?"

"I'm fine. I'll send him up."

"Thank you. The police will be there in three or four minutes."

"Do you want me to stay on the line?"

"No. That's unnecessary. Just send your friend up to the parking lot and have him wait. Call us again if you need to. Thank you."

Elaine turned to her tall 'athletic nerd' friend, recently graduated with some sort of IT degree. "Craig, they want you to go up into the parking lot and bring the cops down here when they arrive." And she hung up.

"I'm on it. I'll be able to see you from up there. Don't worry." Craig knew Elaine could handle anything man or nature could throw at

2

Chapter Two: This doesn't belong

[start here]

The river hadn't been that low in five years. Elaine and Craig, jogging on the path that used to be at the water's edge but was now twenty feet from the river, were talking about that. "So many sand bars," Elaine said. "There's no way even to get our kayaks through that."

"We could probably run right there in the channel," Craig said, spacing his words in between breaths.

"Not in these shoes," she laughed. "Hey, wait! What's that?"

They stopped. "A log? A muddy rock?"

As they walked down to the water, the strange shape came into focus. "It's a package," she said. "It's all tied up with rope… Oh. Oh, crap." She fumbled in the Spandex for her phone.

"Nine-one-one. Please state your emergency."

"I don't know if it's an emergency or not. I'm down by the river, right below the Burger King on East Avenue."

"What is the problem?"

"There's a, a package in the river. It's big, all wrapped up in a blanket or a rug or something,

Caught by a Cat

Contents

her. She was a veteran outdoorswoman, survival camper, a black belt in three disciplines of martial arts, and, although she didn't carry a pistol when she was running, a crack shot. Five-foot-nothing and a hundred and ten pounds, her compact body looked even smaller. But pity anyone who underestimated her.

* * *

"That's it?" the taller of the officers asked.

"That's it," said Craig.

Elaine spoke. "Like I said, I don't know what it is, but it doesn't belong in the river."

The shorter officer said, "Tell me everything."

Elaine was brief. "Well, like I said, we were running on this path here, from over there," she pointed, "when we both saw this… whatever it is. It was so muddy, we didn't notice much, but as we got closer, we could tell it wasn't a rock. And when we saw the ropes around it, we didn't know what to think. But it doesn't belong in the river. That's for sure. That's when I called nine-one-one. And I just waited down here, and Craig went up to the parking lot to wait for you. That's everything."

He turned to Craig, who said, "That's it, officer. That's everything we know."

The shorter one took their contact information, gave them his card, and sent them home. "We've got it from here," he said. "Thank you both."

The taller officer was standing in the river next to the package, and he saw that the ropes passed through a couple concrete cinder blocks. "Hey, Stumpf, we've got a problem here," he called to the officer on shore. Stumpf called the dispatcher and asked for a crime scene team and a detective.

Fred "Tree" Stumpf was forty-three, five-foot-six, built square and close to the ground. A high school All-State wrestler, he still worked out religiously. On the force nearly twenty years and divorced for eighteen, he was known as smart – he knew something about everything, and a lot about a lot of things -- and devoted to his job.

* * *

"I'll have a look around here," Detective Redding said to the photographer and evidence tech, "until you're ready for me." He pulled on his boots, the kind fly fishermen wear, lest he become the victim of a spot of dirt or water. He was a stickler for a sharp appearance.

Behind his back, they called him Mr. Blackwell, but they respected him for his high close rate and attention to details others overlooked. He also had a knack for having the right educated hunch at the right time, something he couldn't explain, but something that everyone knew was real.

He walked along the path in both directions, looking to see where someone would have had the easiest access to the spot where the package was found. *The concrete blocks would have kept the bundle from going very far with the current*, he figured. *It looked like the easiest approach would have been the same way I got there, from the parking lot*. He walked up the same way he arrived, looking for… anything.

The area had a lot of traffic most of the year, when the weather was nice and the trees were green, but he didn't see anyone around. It was warm today, for the end of February, but big snow could still come. It was cold most days.

The river was low, and sticky mud extended several yards from the slow-moving waters, keeping people away from the river itself. Deer and small-animal tracks, yes. People tracks, no.

People stayed on the regular, year-round path, four or five feet higher and a good fifteen feet sideways from where the water trickled, occasional thin ice at its edges.

Redding went up and down the trail to the parking lot. There was plenty of evidence of traffic, but nothing unusual. No deep footprints, no drag marks. No one had brought anything large or heavy through there in a while.

"Okay, Detective, we're ready." The photographer stepped back from the bundle. Redding waded in, the water just above his ankles. He walked slowly around the package, confirming that the photog had shot *this*, and gotten *that* angle.
He finally said, "Let's bring it up where it's dry, and open it up."

They all grabbed the ropes and started pulling together. The rotted rope snapped, Redding lost his balance, slipped on the muddy riverbed, and sat down awkwardly in the water, which poured into his waders. Everyone turned away.

"Well, let's get this up there," he said, gruffly, trying not to laugh at himself, which would have made things much worse among his partners.

This time, they reached under the package to lift, and they all thought the same thing, at the same time: *there's someone in there!*

"Stop," Redding yelled. "Get a body bag. We're going to take this whole thing back to the lab, just as it is." So the disintegrating "blanket, or rug, or something," its contents, fragments of rope, and two cinder blocks all got a ride to the morgue.

***

There, they carefully unwrapped the soggy blanket as mud, smelly water, and hundreds of waterlogged leaves collected in the gutters of thc stainless steel table, and they video'd the whole process.

The body was wrapped in the shreds of a mostly-disintegrated shower curtain liner in the blanket.

The remains were human, but there were no hands. There were no teeth in the skull or jaw, which was broken in two, front and center.

Some sinew remained and held most of the bones in proper relation to the others.

The organs were indistinguishable to Redding, and most of the flesh was either gone or had turned into a gooey slop, barely staying in its original position on or close to the bones.

Skin hung here and there, either lying in the blanket or draped over the bones. The remains of jeans and a collared t-shirt that was probably once white, no belt or buckle – they were there, too.

Redding looked at the Medical Examiner, who shrugged his shoulders. Then he called on his radio to "Get a team down to the river, and find the rest of the parts. We need more of this guy to find out who he is. Or she," he added, rolling his eyes to the ceiling tiles.

He turned back to the ME. "When?"

"Last summer, give or take a couple months. Not more than a year, though. Maybe as late as early October. If you can get the records of the river levels, that may help, too. Too cold right now for parasites. February. The river was all frozen in recent times."

"Thanks, Quincy." Redding was no good at figuring out when was the right time to joke. "When I know something, I'll let you know," said Dr. Hubert Mills, M.D., M.E.

Mills had come to be a Medical Examiner late in his career. When he was fifty, he gave up his practice as a pediatrician. "Sick of the noise," he said, as he commenced the course of study that made him a Medical Examiner. Now sixty-five, he preferred the company of his "patients" to most of the live people with whom he worked.

* * *

Jerry Redding returned to his office to start a file and wait for some results from the morgue or the team that was searching the river. *What is this? No hands, no teeth. Was it somebody who was already missing one, or who had some abnormality? They could have cut them all off, just to keep us from figuring that out. No teeth, no dental records. Kinda rough on the jaw – did they break the jaw getting the teeth out?*

Then he thought something that turned his stomach. *Did they do this before death, after – or as part of it? Christ. Who hates anybody that much?*

He looked through the missing persons reports from March through October of last year. *Gotta start somewhere.*

Ruling out the few very short-stature missing persons, Redding was left with forty men and seventeen women still missing, from the five-county area. Most were from the big city to the south. Only five – three men and two women – were local, and had disappeared before November, during last year.

He picked up the phone and dialed the extension for Records. "Hi, Connie? It's Jerry. Say, can you give me missing persons from the year before last, too?... Yes, this might be a longer-term thing, a kidnapping maybe... Whatever you've got. Thanks." *Well, that will uncomplicate things.*

Connie brought in three more files. Two – a man and a woman, missing over the previous year – were potential victims. *Unless our body is from somewhere else, we've got seven. And once we find out if it's male or female, no more than four.* He waited for news from the ME's office as he studied all seven files.

* * *

Redding picked up his ringing desk phone. "Hello, Detective Redding. It's Doctor Mills. I have something that may help."

"Thank you, Doctor Mills. What you got?"

"'Doctor Mills?' Give me a break, Jerry." The faked forced formality was over. "This may be good. The jeans? Size six, expensive."

"So, we most likely have a female victim. Anything else?"

"She had two broken ribs on her right side. Fresh breaks."

"Peri- or post-mortem?"

"There looks to be blood in one of the breaks. That could be an indication that they were broken during whatever event killed her. We're running some more tests to see if I'm right. But these aren't nearly enough to be cause of death."

"So you have a cause of death?"

"Likelier that it's related to her cracked skull. Both breaks are right at or just after death; there's no remodeling… er, healing on any of them. Most-likely COD is from having her hands cut off."

"She died in a fight, then? Any wounds from weapons?"

"The cuts on her lower arms are clean. Chops. Teeth were definitely pulled, and she had all of them except her wisdom teeth. The rest is just blunt force, difficult to categorize… We're still trying to make sense of the hair and the rest of the clothes. The blanket and rope may give us some more clues. Just getting started here. I'll get everything to your guys at the police lab as soon as I do my work."

"Thanks, Hugh."

"One more thing, Jerry. Don't know if it's significant."

"Everything's significant at this stage of the game. What?"

"That blanket. It's a blanket, not a rug. Wool. Lots of cat hairs on it."

"That's it? Okay. Get as many as you can. See if you can tell if they're from the same cat. Bag 'em. You never know."

"Will do. Just thought you'd want to know."

"Thanks." Cat hairs? *Maybe a cat killed her. Maybe a whole cat gang. Vicious nasty felines. Maybe a lion. Now, that would be cool.* Jerry instinctively brushed himself off as he walked back to his office.

* * *

"Detective Redding? This is Detective Johnny Johnson, Asheville PD. that's Asheville, North Carolina."

"This is Jerry Redding. What can I do for you?"

"Well, I may have something for you. We've recovered a stolen car from your area. A three-year-old Lexus."

"Well, Thank you, Detective. But why call me? Why not just run it through regular channels?"

"Because it's a little special. Pro job. VIN plate switch. Newer Lexus and all. Doesn't show up as stolen, but we traced the real VIN to your area."

"A stolen Lexus that hasn't been reported stolen? Okay, go on. What did you get from the VIN?"

"It was sold new by Argyle Lexus, to a Jean A. Leitner, 36 Carriage Park Drive."

Redding butted in. "Yeah, I know the place. Got it." Redding was suddenly intense.

Johnson continued, irked by the interruption, "We don't have BMV records on registrations in your state, so I don't know if she's still the owner."

"Thanks, er… Johnson. Give me what you've got. I'm ready." Redding took notes as Asheville's Johnny Johnson gave him the details.

When the call was over, he yelled through his open door. "Stumpf! Get your arse in here!"

Fred Stumpf appeared at Redding's desk. "Yeah, I'm here. What's up? There's decent people trying to sleep out there."

His joke was ignored. "The name Jean Leitner ring a bell?"

"Isn't she the young widow, the missing suspect, the one who killed her husband?"

"Well, I don't think she's just a suspect any more. And I don't think she's missing. I think she's dead."

"What's up? Where do I fit in?"

"It's nothing but a hunch at this moment, but I think it's a good one. Remember that body in the river, the one in the blanket, that those runners found? I'm going to bet we've got Jean Leitner, the late Mrs. David John Moore Leitner, neé Richardson, in the cooler across the street."

"Is she in Missing Persons?"

"No, and that's one reason why none of 'em matches our body. We were figuring she offed her husband and flew the coop. This would also explain why we haven't seen a trace of her or her car."

"Back up a minute," Stumpf said. "I'm missing something. I thought Mrs. Leitner killed her rich old husband with an overdose of insulin, and took off for parts unknown."

"So did I, except she didn't drain any accounts, and she didn't claim his insurance. We figured she'd been stashing little chunks of dough away and was waiting until we caught somebody else for the murder, to come out of hiding and make her claim. Since she was hiding, it made sense that her phone and credit cards had gone dark, too."

"What you got, now?" said a confused Stumpf. "And why are you telling me?"

"I'm all on hunches for now, and I don't want to talk to anybody who matters when all I've got are hunches, but I have to know if this makes any sense."

"Thanks a lot."

"No, Tree, you don't understand. Not a put-down. I respect your analytical mind. I just have to bounce this around a bit until the

14

pieces make sense, 'cuz It doesn't make sense. She died a violent death, and he didn't have a mark on him. He died in his sleep."

"So she didn't die from a fight with him."

"Right. But he's still dead, and probably on the same day that she disappeared."

"So, she stuck him, turned around, and fell down the stairs."

"Yeah," Redding said, "and pulled out her own teeth, cut off her hands, wrapped herself in a shower curtain and a blanket, tied herself to a couple cinder blocks, and jumped into the river, just to screw with us."

"Okay, probably not. So somebody killed both of them."

"Or – and this is way out there -- she killed the old man and then somebody jumped *her*."

Stumpf scratched his head. "But we don't know if that's her in the blanket."

"Right. We need Quincy to make that phone ring." And just then, the phone rang. "Redding."

"Jerry, it's Mills." Redding motioned for Fred to sit down, and put the call on speaker. Stumpf moved closer to Jerry's desk. "What you got?"

"Don't take it to the bank yet, but our victim in the blanket could very well be Jean Leitner."

"When will you know?"

"Now that I've got a good place to start, I can look for things that match up. I'm not going to stand behind this formally, but I think you can stop looking for our pretty young suspect on the run."

"Thanks, Hugh. Let me know when you're sure. I won't say anything for now. But I'll get started on it as if we both know."

"It won't be long, if she's not our victim. It'll be a couple days to confirm if she is."

"Just keep me up to date. You've given me pretty much a whole new case. Thanks a lot for that, buddy."

"Happy to help. I'll call you with the official stuff, real soon." And he hung up.

Stumpf and Redding looked at the speaker on his desk, as if the phone would ring again. "Well, we open one door, we get a whole new look at things," said Redding, as Stumpf slowly walked back to his desk. "Kee-ryst," he said aloud, to no one.

* * *

The Lexus had been sold in Atlanta, under a salvage title, with a windshield VIN tag from a wrecked car, same year and color. Cars carry their VINs (vehicle identification numbers) in at least two places, and only the windshield

16

location is commonly known. The "secret VIN" or "hidden VIN," stamped in different locations on different models, is used, principally by law enforcement, for verification, and its existence and location are not public knowledge.

The car's windshield VIN plate, maybe the whole dashboard, instruments and all, had been swapped from a wreck, and a crooked dealer got a salvage title for it under that VIN.

But the crooked dealer had not swapped out the firewall from the wreck. So that number matched the real car, Jean Leitner's car.

The mismatch was discovered by chance. A veteran officer was showing a rookie how to double-check VINs on a suspicious car. As the veteran read the firewall VIN, the rookie read the windshield VIN (which matched the registration), and when they didn't match each other, the hapless driver of the Lexus got a ride to the station, where he explained what he knew.

* * *

Redding had his chin in one hand and that elbow on his cluttered desk. He cleared a space with his other elbow, and put his head in his hands and stared at the wall. *So, our theory about Mister DJM Leitner's death may be no good, and our theory about little gold-digging Jean Leitner's sudden invisibility is blown up, and we now have no suspects and no motive, and the murderer or murderers have maybe a nine-month head start. Is it five o'clock yet? I need a drink. Hell, it's five o'clock somewhere, right?*

And he retrieved the bottle of Jim Beam from the bottom drawer of his desk and put it square in front of him. Not that he checked, or that it would have mattered, but it was a quarter to five.

* * *

Redding pulled out the slim file on David Leitner, and a new yellow legal pad, and he started to write.

 •Motive?
 •Suspects?
 •Opportunity?
 •Background?

And he left space under each one.

Since Jean is dead, relatives will be coming out of the woodwork to make claims on the estate. What's at stake? Who gains the most? Who's first at the door, blood or in-laws?

Jerry thought of calling Leitner's family lawyer. *Better wait until we know for sure Jean's dead.* He wrote some more.

Then he dialed internally, to Records. "Connie? Jerry. What do we have on David Leitner, the insulin murder last September? Anything at all?"

"Hi, Jerry. Ummm… Just a second… Got him here. Well, he was fifty-eight, married four years to Jean. Both, their second marriages. She was twenty-six at the time. When he died, he ran six laundromats here, two more in the Heights."

"Yeah, the Brighty Whities. I remember. Can't forget."

"Anyway, he went bankrupt at forty, when he was a loan officer at Plowman's Credit Union. Three brothers. Jim, now sixty-three if he's alive – we don't have anything on him at all; Shane, lives in the Heights, forty-eight; ran those two laundromats. Now he runs them all.

"Middle brother Rick is fifty. He's gay and he went off on a world tour with his partner two years ago.

"Nothing since he left. David's first wife is Elizabeth, divorced after two years of marriage, when they both were twenty-four. She lives 'out east.' We're narrowing that down. No kids, from either marriage."

"That's good. Can you get me something on that bankruptcy?"

"I'll see what I can find on the bankruptcy."

"And what about his wife, Jean?"

"Jean's file is not much. She's thirty. Widowed at twenty-four; Leitner was the second marriage for her, too. No kids. Former 'Miss Island Tan,'" and Connie laughed a little.

"What's funny?"

"It was San Juan Island."

"What's funny about that? There's plenty of sun in Puerto Rico."

"Jerry, San Juan Island is north of Seattle, between the mainland and Vancouver Island. San Juan Island is a rain forest. You couldn't get a tan there if…"

"Okay, very funny. What else?"

"We don't have anything much on her."

"Well, just bring me what you have, and let's start looking at Leitner's bank records. Let's get a financial profile on the guy."

"Sure. When do you need it?"

"Is yesterday okay? We're half a year behind, at least. Thanks, Connie. Have a good weekend." And Redding looked at the clock that showed three minutes 'til five. Close enough. He unscrewed the cap and took a drink.

Chapter Three: Barry Cassidy

Daylight Saving Time had kicked in overnight, so Jerry Redding's Sunday morning walk along the river, down below the Burger King, wasn't in full daylight. *They could have just backed up in the parking lot, and the trunk would have been nearly invisible behind the bushes and leaves up there. Getting the body down, easy. You could even roll it, but dragging would be better. More control.*

He walked up to the parking lot and guessed the best, the most-shielded spot for the car to back in. He looked downhill from there.

What's the path of least resistance here? He sidestepped down the muddy, dead leaf covered slope, making mental notes. Then he went back up, and tried an alternate route. *No, the first one, for sure. But those rocks – could they have broken a rib, cracked a skull?* He froze, a chill in his soul. *Could those bastards have cut her up, still alive?*

Detective Jerry Redding, veteran of more than eighty homicide investigations, walked over to a slight depression in the river's bank, among the bare branches of some bush, and threw up.

* * *

On Monday morning, Redding couldn't wait any more. "Hugh, I had a horrible thought. Could she – Jean Leitner – have died from bleeding out? From having her hands cut off? Could she have been still alive when she was wrapped up, and the broken ribs and cracked head wound happen when she was in the blanket? Is that even possible?"

"Jerry, where'd you get that idea? Let me think… God, that's awful. You really need help. But, well, there'd be a lot of blood trace in the package, for sure. Probably, anyway."

"But she was in the river over six months."

"Yeah, but… let me look at the blanket a little closer. Not my job to say, but I don't like how you think, Jerry."

"Truth is all I want. And for the record, I don't want this to be what happened, okay?"

"Understood."

"And is that Jean Leitner?"

"I'll know before lunch. 'Bye, ya weirdo."

* * *

At half past one, Mills finally called. "Jerry, it's Leitner. Positive."

"Well, thanks. That's a big one. I'll get started."

"Jerry, wait. There's more."

"Can we do the rest, later this afternoon?"

22

"Sure. She's not going to get any deader. It's important, but it can wait a couple hours. But not 'til tomorrow."

"I promise I'll call you as soon as I get… this off my desk." And he hung up and immediately called Barry Cassidy, Esq.

Cassidy, thirty-four years old, was the family attorney for the late Leitners. Raised locally, he had been a friend of Jean Leitner's for some years, and her lawyer since her first husband's passing. When David Leitner's lifelong attorney, Mel McGowan, died, Jean convinced him to bring on Cassidy, rather than stay with McGowan's super-stodgy old firm, Erickson and Eckersoll.

Flashy, long-haired, and full of himself, Cassidy handled a small number of high net worth accounts, largely due to the influence of one of his clients, a Mr. Clarence "Chip" Pullman, a private investor who had pulled out of the markets just before they crashed and then re-invested on President Obama's inauguration day, when they were near their lows.

His slightly more than modest fortune in 2009 had made him the richest man in town today, and his practice of loaning money locally made his one-man home-based business the topic of much speculation, even as it collected allies. And debtors.

Pullman first got involved with Cassidy over Cassidy's writeup in the local paper almost twenty years ago, when the high-schooler was noticed as a star swimmer who also had the best GPA in the school, and who had just scored a perfect 800 on the SAT test. Cassidy, the story pointed out, was the oldest of nine children being raised by a single mom, and could see no way to afford college away from home.

So Pullman approached Barry's mom and made a deal with young Cassidy, promising him financial help as long as he maintained his GPA in high school. When Cassidy became valedictorian, Pullman announced he would finance his college, a year at a time, anywhere he could get into, as long as he kept up his grades. The young man stayed on track and graduated at the top of his class at difficult Grand Canyon University in Arizona.

Cassidy dropped out of organized sports in college, but he maintained his personal training, and retained the build of a weightlifting diver, compact, taut, and with defined and over-large muscles. "But that's just because I like to exercise," he said. "I just don't have time for all the organized stuff." He claimed exercise helped build his stamina… for studying.

Well, Cassidy wanted to go to law school, and wrangled a partial scholarship from Northwestern University's School of Law in Chicago. Not enough of a scholarship, but it was a great school. And Pullman offered again. This time, though, it was not a gift, but a private student loan, on the condition that Cassidy, whatever his future in the law, would be on Pullman's team.

So Cassidy went to Northwestern, where he graduated in the top twenty percent of his class and then, surprisingly, went into private practice in his home town, doing all the things local lawyers do – wills, pre-nuptials and divorces, taxes, contracts, and some minor criminal work, whenever a local got into trouble that wasn't big trouble.

Now he was a mid-thirties small-time star, enjoying the single life of a shiny fish in a smallish pond.

And Chip Pullman helped build Cassidy's rep, sending his friends to him whenever they needed delicate help with things that they didn't want their regular law firms to know about. Barry Cassidy kept secrets and handled matters discreetly, and was well-compensated for that. And he never charged Clarence or Vanessa Pullman a dime, ever.

* * *

"Mister Cassidy, I'm Detective Jerry Redding. I'm afraid I have some bad news for you."

"This is Barry Cassidy. What news?"

"We have just received confirmation that your client, Jean Leitner, is dead."

"Oh. Uhh…" Redding heard Cassidy choke up a little. "Detective, what's this about? When did it happen? Where is she?"

"When did you hear from her last, if I may ask?"

"Uhh, actually, it's been quite some time. I'm thinking, since Mister Leitner died. Last… September or thereabouts."

"Think, now. Did you hear from her – at all -- since David Leitner died?"

"Now that you mention it, no. And I thought that was strange. But tell me how she died. Where is she?"

"She's in the morgue, here in town, and we don't know how she died, but it's been a while since she was killed."

"Killed? What? How? Who did it?" Then Redding heard Cassidy's voice, straining for control. "Can I help?"

Redding wrote some notes in his yellow pad, and said, "I would really appreciate if you could come down to the station and tell me whatever you know. Confidentiality respected, of course."

"Thank you. I can come right now," said Barry Cassidy. "Would that work?"

"I'm on the second floor. Tell them at the desk you're here to see me."

* * *

Barry Cassidy, flushed and out of breath, arrived with a police sergeant at Redding's door, ten minutes later. He looked like he had been crying.

Redding looked up. "Mister Cassidy?" Barry nodded. "Please have a seat. Would you like some coffee? A soft drink?"

Cassidy said, "Thank you. I'm not thirsty," and took his seat across Redding's desk, back to the door.

The room was about the size of a trade-show booth, maybe ten feet square, made considerably smaller by the large metal desk in its center. The window was behind Redding, bright afternoon sun silhouetting him.

There was a paper shredder at one end of the desk. *It'll never hold all this crap,* Cassidy thought, looking at the piles of papers on the desk and the foot-high stacks of files all over the rest of the floor.

I bet this place hasn't been vacuumed in ten years. Certificates and framed, mostly black-and-white photos covered one side wall. The other side wall had a large cork board with half a jillion unidentifiable notes and a few pictures tacked to it. Redding casually got up, walked to the cork board, and closed its doors.

Cassidy didn't notice what was on the wall behind him. When the sergeant shut the door, Cassidy had the feeling that there wasn't enough air for two in the room. He immediately regretted having turned down the soda.

"What happened to Jean?" the young lawyer asked.

"I'm sorry for your loss. I understand she was your friend as well as your client," Redding offered, sincerely.

"Yes. Really, a friend, mostly." He asked again, "What happened to her?"

Redding replied, "I'll tell you what I can, but first, I have some questions I'd like to ask you. If you feel I'm asking things that are covered by attorney-client privilege, I certainly don't want you to compromise your legal ethics, but I would also like to ask for some of your personal knowledge, which isn't protected. Of course, I can't compel you to answer anything, but I trust you'd like to help solve this case as much as I do."

"Certainly. Please, please tell me what happened."

"In good time, Mister Cassidy. Now, how long have you known the deceased. Err… Jean Leitner?"

"Jean and I go back to when she was in high school. Fifteen years, about. I was just out. We met the summer after my freshman year in Arizona."

"Grand Canyon?"

"Yes. How did you know that?"

"Business major?"

"General management. How?"

"Isn't that mostly a girls' school?"

"It's known for nursing. I went for business. And because I hate winter weather."

"Then to Northwestern for law school?"

"You know that, too."

"By then, you liked Chicago winters?"

"No. By then, I wanted to go to law school, and that was the best, closest one."

"Closest… to?"

"Closest to my mother." Redding raised that eyebrow again. "And to Jean, yes."

"Expensive."

"I had a scholarship."

"It's expensive, living in Chicago, too,

especially on the near north side, especially by the lake. How'd you do it? Part-time job?"

"I got a loan. Lived in a rented room in Evanston. That's…"

"I know where Evanston is. Your loan, from?"

"From Mister Chip Pullman. He paid for my high school and most of my college. You know that, too. And yes, now I'm his lawyer. Why all this about me? What happened to Jean?"

Redding changed tack. "Okay, let's talk about Missus Leitner, Miss Richardson. And you. Tell me all about you. Her. Both of you, together." Cassidy flushed. *Anger or embarrassment?* Redding wondered. *This might get interesting.*

"Well, I'll get the romance out of the way, first. We dated. She was in high school. I was in college. Then she got married, and I went to law school, finished law school, got married myself. Then we both got divorced, and we started dating again, but mostly just for old times' sake."

Redding thought, *She was widowed. What's up? Did he know her, or what? Is he just distraught? Deal with it later…* "How serious were you at each of these times?"

30

"Oh, at first we were way serious." He looked straight at Redding. "She was a virgin when we started dating."

"And when you went back to school that fall?"

He smirked. Unseemly. "She wasn't."

Redding closeted his growing disgust and regrouped. "Then, between, when both of you were divorced?"

"Yes, we were intimate, but we didn't make plans for the future, like we did when we were young."

"And then she married David Leitner, and you just walked away?"

"Yes. Well, that way, yes. A couple years ago, when his forever lawyer died, she introduced us. Well, she endorsed me, and I became his lawyer. Their lawyer."

"What was your relationship with the Leitners last September?"

"At the end, we were friends, Jean and I. We always were. David and I had a solid business relationship. Professional relationship, as attorney and client."

"Did he know your, ummm, history with Jean?"

"I doubt it, beyond friendship, you mean – I mean. Unless she told him. And she never told me that she told him."

"One more thing: can you think of anyone who would want to harm her? Or David, for that matter?"

"David was – you know this, too – a small-time loan shark. Maybe a money launderer, but I can't give you any more than that. There were probably a few people who didn't like him. Jean? As far as I was concerned, she was an angel. Now will you tell me what happened to her?"

Redding stood up, pushed in his chair, and walked a step to his left, then a couple steps back. It was all he could do, to approximate pacing. "I can't tell you much, since it's a murder investigation, as I mentioned over the phone. She was found last week, in the river. Her body had been… abused. We don't have much to go on."

Then, "I really thank you for coming in." And he walked to the door and opened it. "You know the way. If you think of anything useful, please share it with me."

"Like you opened your soul to me. Sure," he said, darkly. And he disappeared down the staircase.

Redding was glad to leave the office door open. After that interview, there was no air left.

* * *

"Okay, Hugh. Back to you as promised. What 'cha got for me?" Redding's mood had improved since Cassidy left his office. *Little slimeball. He's not going to share a damn thing.*

"Well, it's bad. I did some really close looking, and I believe that at least one of the ribs was broken peri-mortem."

"So, she was in a fight. We kinda figured that, right?"

"And her right hand was removed while she was still alive, too. Maybe her left hand, too. Maybe her teeth. I just don't have enough to go on. But I'm ninety-nine percent sure of the right hand and the one rib. Her head injury was post-mortem."

"How?"

"We don't know about the rib. Her hand was severed, chopped off in a single blow, by a sharp instrument."

"An axe?"

"Sharper than your average axe. Could be an axe, but more likely, a knife. Heavy knife, like a cleaver or a machete. Maybe even a sword – no serration marks, that's important to know. Sharper than your average axe. Much sharper. Almost no crush damage, all slice."

A chill went up Redding's spine. "Oh, lord. The other hand?"

"Clean. Same kind of thing. Huge amount of force on a very sharp blade. Because the cuts are so clean, the blood thoroughly washed away. No conclusive case for peri- or post. The shower curtain, the blanket – nothing at all."

"Is that possible? There must have been a ton of blood."

"All that time in the river, yes. Possibly also they washed her off before they wrapped her up."

"Maybe in a bathtub? Maybe that's why the shower curtain?"

"You're the detective, Jerry."

"The head wound?"

"Jerry, I believe that was post-mortem. You asked about rough handling on the way down to the river. I think that might be the explanation for the broken skull. As for the ribs, certainly one broke while she was alive, but compared to everything else, it's minor. Probably from the initial confrontation. I'm calling cause of death exsanguination. She bled to death. I'll write this up, send the photos. Then it'll all be yours."

"Thanks, Hugh. I think I'm gonna be sick. Then I'm gonna find that bastard."

"Take care, Jerry."

34

Redding leaned back in his chair and took a breath. *I don't really give a shit what time it is.* And he reached down to his lower-left drawer for his rich oak-colored 80-proof friend, Jim Beam.

Chapter Four: A shower curtain

Tuesday morning, Redding went to the Leitners' old house. The estate had received permission to rent it out in mid-October; the crime scene team was done with it.

The door was opened by a forty-ish brunette, plain but attractive. "Hello?"

"Hello, ma'am." Holding up his badge and motioning with his head toward the police car in front of the house, he continued, "I'm Detective Jerry Redding, and I regret the intrusion, but I have a few questions I'd like to ask you about your house here. May I come in?"

"Sure. Okay." She stepped aside. "I'm Gina Verdad. Carlos is at work. He's my husband. I just made coffee…"

Redding nodded. "Thank you, black, please."

She led the way to the living room and motioned for Redding to take one of the comfortable overstuffed chairs, which he recognized from the crime scene photos. "You rented this place already furnished? When?" Gina returned, coffee mug and napkin in hand. "Yes. Furnished. We signed the lease for November, but we got to move in the weekend before, at the end of October. We were lucky about the furniture. We liked everything here and it's part of the lease. Everything's the same as before, except..."

Redding raised an eyebrow.

"Except," she continued, looking suddenly distant, "the mattresses upstairs. In the room where…"

"Where the man died?"

Her vacant look was gone as fast as it had appeared, replaced again by a bright visage. "Yes. The mattresses are new. But it was great. All we had to do was move in. We didn't need to buy a stick of furniture."

"Did you remodel anything? Anything at all?"

"Well, we changed the curtains in the guest bedroom. That's all, I guess."

"Think really hard, Miss Verdad." Redding couldn't pronounce Ms. "Did you change the shower curtains?"

"Shower curtains?" She thought a moment. "No. They're all the same."

Redding's hunch was no good. But she perked up and continued.
"But – yes -- we did buy a new liner for the guest bath. Funny, all the other curtains had a liner, but not that one. Maybe the guest room

was more or less just for show. Or maybe they always bought new ones. Those things trap moisture and get black, even if you only use them once, if there's any moisture in them at all."

"Interesting. Hey, have you used that bathroom since you moved in?"

"No. All I did was put up a new liner, like I said. Why do you ask?"

"Strange request: could I have that shower curtain? The cloth one, not the liner?"

"They're expensive."

"Okay, could I buy it from you? Twenty dollars?"

She smiled. "Forty?"

"Sold. Do you have a plastic bag I could put it in?"

They went to the guest bathroom and helped each other take down the shower curtain, as the detective looked around for other clues: chipped porcelain, maybe a bent shower curtain rod. "Did you say these aren't the original drapes?" he asked.

"Yes, these are new. The old ones were torn at the edge. And, oh yes, we also replaced the curtain rod. The old one was sagging."

"Sagging?"

"Yes, some of the screws were pulled out of the wall, at that end, there. So we redid it. Works fine now."

"And they're fine looking drapes, too," Redding added. "All the furniture's the same, though, and in the same places as when you moved in?"

"We never come in here. So, yes."

"One last thing, Miss Verdad. Are the other shower liners original with the house, as you moved in?" She nodded. "Could I look at them, too?"

"You redoing your house?"

"No. Just curious. And I'd like to take a picture of them with my cell phone, if that's okay with you."

"You can have them for ten dollars apiece." She laughed.

He laughed, too. "No, thanks. Just pictures."

She took him to the other bathrooms, where he was pleased to see that all the shower curtain liners matched. He took pictures of them all – eyelets and hems, particularly. "Well, thank you for the coffee, and the shower curtain, Miss Verdad. You drive a hard bargain, but I'm sure you'll enjoy your new one."
She smiled. "If you want anything else, feel free to come back and shop."

"Good day, Miss Verdad." And she shut the door as soon as he stepped out. *How am I going to get reimbursed for that?* he thought, as he tossed the shower curtain in the Walmart bag, onto the passenger seat of the car.

* * *

At the police lab, Redding handed the bag to Artie, a sharp young lab tech who, Redding thought, made more of his tech school training than half the doctors he knew did of medical school.

"Hi, Artie," he said. "I've got a project for you. Somewhere on this shower curtain is some blood or evidence of some blood. I'd like you to find it, document it, and if you can, see what else you can find out. Probably no DNA, but maybe we can get a blood type on it."

"Sure, Detective," his smiling eyes bright in his Ethiopian, nearly blue-black face. "Where is it?" he asked, as he turned the curtain over in his latex-gloved hands. "The blood?"

"Well, Artie, that's the tough part. I don't know. You'll have to find it yourself."

"And you're sure it's on here?"

"Positive. Let's see what you can do."

"Okay, Detective Redding. Just sign it in." And he pushed the clipboard with the forms across the counter. "I'll get right to it."

Chapter Five: Old tech still works

Detective Jerry Redding was checking his inter-office mail. Artie sent a short message with an attachment.

> Det. Redding, I couldn't find anything by eye, but ultraviolet light showed some tiny drops along this one edge (see attached). DNA unlikely. Maybe there's enough there to get a type. More later.
> Artie

How that kid can even see this is beyond me. Look at that – it looks like dust on the lens, if that.

Redding dialed the lab. "Hi, Artie. Redding. Listen, good work on that shower curtain."

"Detective? We just found out it's O-positive. I hope that helps."

"O-positive? You're sure?"

"One hundred percent, sir. Positive."

"Thank you, Artie. Good work."

"You're welcome, Detective. Thank you, too."

It's a match to Jean. So what does that tell us? Why just tiny drops? If they were chopping off her hand, it ought to be a gusher.

He thought some more. *How could that gusher leave such tiny drops?* Then it hit him.

Oh, yeah, the gusher hit the liner. This is spatter on the curtain. Duh, Redding!

I wish the evidence team had looked in the other rooms more thoroughly. We got nothing from the guest suite. No pictures, no reports of water or blood in the bathtub. Nobody noticed the liner was gone from the tub and the curtains were torn at the window. Curtain rod pulled halfway out of the wall, nobody saw it. Nothing. Bupkis.

Chapter Six: A beautiful friendship

Redding lay in bed, unable to sleep. *I've got all I'm gonna get. We thought she killed him and took off, but she's dead, and likely at the same time. Same day at least. Same morning. The points are where they should be, and the syringes are in the garbage. That's the wife's work. A pro wouldn't have left them in the house.*
So, she killed him. Why? And why was she killed, and so brutally? How did she get someone that mad at her? Who did she know that was so crazy, so primitive? Local, probably. It would take a while for an out-of-towner to find that dump spot behind the Burger King. How did her car end up in Atlanta?
Redding went over these thoughts and many others until about three in the morning. When the alarm went off at six-thirty, he felt miserable.
* * *

"Stumpf, can you stop making all that noise over there? And congratulations on the promotion, by the way."
"Shove it, Redding," he said jokingly. "Moving into a new office is gonna make some noise. And it's *Detective* Stumpf to you!"

"Long time coming, friend. I'm glad they
finally figured you out. You deserve it."

"Yeah, I know, right? Thanks." The newly-
promoted Detective Fred "Tree" Stumpf
looked out his window, the first window he'd
ever had in the first office he'd ever had, after
eighteen years of assignments in nearly every
area of the PD. "So, guess what my first case
assignment is?"

"Finding Waldo?"

"No, jerk. Finding the Leitner killer. You've
got a partner."

"Or killers," Redding said, serious. "I could
use some help. Welcome aboard."

"So, what do we have?" he asked Redding,
as the two went to the cafeteria to get some
tall coffees.

Redding spelled it out. "Our early theory,
that Jean killed her old man and then took off,
is wrong. I'm of the strong belief that she
killed him, all right. But I don't understand
why, or why she was killed. Or by whom."

"What about the nest egg she was putting
aside for her escape?" asked the shorter man.

"We haven't found it. We're looking through
her card receipts and checks. We hadn't paid
them much attention, since we believed in the

theory and were spending time looking for her."

"And the old man's finances?"

"David's accounts were a mess, particularly considering he used to work as a loan officer at that bank."

"Credit union."

"Right – good catch. Credit union. A lot of money went into those laundromats, and there's little evidence that it did anything."

"Laundering more than clothes? How much?"

"Looks like he was, and over a hundred grand a year. Lately, close to two."

"Where'd it go, then?"

"You're gonna make a helluva detective, Tree."

"How many times I gotta tell you, that's *Detective* Tree to you, sir?" And they walked back to their offices.

* * *

The lawyer answered the phone. "This is Barry Cassidy."

"Hello, Mr. Cassidy. It's Detective Redding. I wonder if you could come down to the station again. There's someone here I'd like you to meet."

"Uhhh… Sure. Who's that? Always glad to help. When do you need me?"

"Now is good, if you can break away for half an hour or so."

"How about one-thirty? I'm meeting a client for lunch, and I have to prepare."

"That's fine. You know how to find me. Thanks."

Redding turned to Stumpf, who was looking through the now much-thicker Leitner file, looking for aspects he could handle, to take the load off Redding, the lead detective on the case. "He'll be here about one-thirty. In the meantime, see if you can find out how that car ended up in Atlanta. Start with Johnny Johnson, in Asheville. He's got a lot on that case."

"Anything else?"

"Yeah. Get Connie to make you a set of all the records she's got, and ask her if the two missing brothers – the older one and the gay one – have shown up anywhere. There's a million dollars in insurance just waiting to get paid out."

"Would you like me to prove the Riemann hypothesis, too? Before lunch, I mean?"

"The what? Yeah, sure. Get out of here."

* * *

Cassidy was on time. They used Stumpf's office, not to make him feel important or included, but because, even though it was a mess from the morning's move-in, there was still room in there for three people. More room than Redding had.

Redding made introductions, and all sat down. Then he began: "We need a little help with your client. Again."

"Of course," Cassidy replied. "Anything at all." He paused, and the detective said nothing. "I was a little too tight before, I guess. Sorry about that. With just learning of Jean's death…"

"She meant a lot to you, then?"

"Yes."

"More than just a client." Redding wasn't asking, really. More like he was saying what he already knew.

Cassidy's startled look lasted only a microsecond. He composed himself and said, "There were times when we dated, yes."

Redding played a hunch. "Like since she was in high school, married or not." Again, like he already knew.

"I'm not at liberty to say," and how he said it was all the confirmation the detective needed.

"Look, Mr. Cassidy, you are the common link among the victims, the laundromats, the personal relationship; and you were even in a relationship with the victim at the time of the murders. You're our best source of information to help us solve these. You want to know what happened to your little lover, don't you?"

Cassidy stiffened. "You're fishing. You're prying. Worse, you're asking me to compromise my ethics as a lawyer. Am I a suspect? Do I need a lawyer?"

Stumpf, silent until now, entered the conversation as the good cop. "Chill out, Barry. Just breathe. I understand how you feel. Detective Redding here has been on this case for over a month, and he's getting frustrated. Me? I'm new to it. Why don't you just bring me up to date, everything you can think of? Before, during their marriage, his laundromats. And how was their marriage? And – his businesses were doing well on paper, but he had no money. Do you have any insight you could share with us on that?"

Cassidy squirmed in his chair, stalling.

Stumpf turned to Redding. "Jerry, could you get us some sodas, please?" He turned to Cassidy. "Diet okay?" Cassidy nodded. Redding glowered and left.

Fred resumed. "Look, we don't have much time here. You were lovers, right? The whole time, maybe ten years."

Cassidy was off-guard. He nodded.

"And that's how you got to be Leitner's lawyer?"

"Yes, after McGowan passed away. Jean…"

"And how well did you understand Leitner's business?"

"I was his only lawyer, as far as I know, and he kept his own books. So moderately well, I'd say."

"So why didn't he have any money? The front end of his business looked healthy. Did he have a gambling problem? Drugs? A mistress? What?"

"I'm really trying to help, here, and still be lawyer for his estate. You understand?" Stumpf nodded. Cassidy continued. "I can't imagine his having a mistress. They were both in love, and they were both home most of the time, anyway."

"Even though you and Jean…?"

"Yeah. Uhh, that was mostly habit, convenience, stress release – whatever you'd call it. We enjoyed it, we were good friends, but we weren't in love any more. Drugs? I'm guessing you did a tox screen on him, and I'd bet you didn't find anything in him – or even in the house – that wasn't a vitamin pill or insulin. And gambling? If he did, I didn't know anything about it. David was a straight shooter, devoted, in love with his wife."

"So…?"

"So, dammit, I don't know. I don't know who'd want to kill him. And I sure don't know who'd want to kill Jean. She was so…"

"You still have feelings for her, don't you?"

Redding came back. "Two diets. Need anything else? Cookies, Croissants? Shall I have the chef make something up?" Mock hostility, and they all understood.

"Thanks," Cassidy said, popping open the can. "Ice?" And they all laughed just a little. Redding picked it up. "So we've figured that David Leitner had some kind of drain on finances that he didn't want Jean to know about. Her spending, if anything, increased in the past year or so. If she knew what was bothering him, it'd be hard to imagine she'd increase her spending."

Knowing looks all around, so Redding continued. "So, what did you come up with, while I was running my errand?" Smile. Stumpf said, "We're pretty sure it wasn't the classics – drugs, mistress, gambling." Cassidy nodded. "So I'm left with maybe a secret account. Maybe he was stashing money away for some kind of vacation or big payoff, or…"

"Or extortion," Cassidy volunteered, surprising himself and the detectives.

"Or extortion," Redding confirmed. "A helluva lot of money to hide from the wifey."

"Did she ever talk to you about anything like this?" he asked Cassidy.

"Well, that would be privileged information," he said. "But no, she didn't."

Redding abruptly ended the meeting. "Thank you, Mister Cassidy. If you think of anything else, please let us know."

"Oh, I will. I'm as interested in this case as you guys are." Everyone turned toward the door, and Cassidy left.

* * *

Redding went back to his office, and Stumpf caught up on email. The Lexus had been sold to the Atlanta dealer on a salvage title. "The Lexus came out of Chicago to Atlanta in a wholesale deal," he shouted to Redding. "Looks like the conversion happened in Chicago."

"When?" Redding shouted back.
"Less than a week after David's murder, so our killers likely came out of Chi-town, and

they're connected to some sophisticated car-theft people."

"Good work, Fred. Now get me their names and we can go home."

Connie, who was carrying a box of paper to Redding's office, chimed in. "Now, boys!"

She put the papers on Redding's desk. "Two years of bank statements from Leitner's personal bank, his laundromat bank, and a little joint account he and Jean had. Plus Jean's personal account. Credit card statements, too. And I got a credit report from when she bought the Lexus three years ago."

"How did you…" Redding started to ask.

"I just did, Okay? Do you want it?"

"Ummm… okay, I guess." Then with a smile in his eye, he said, "Thank you, Connie. You're the best."

"Yes, I am," she said, "and I am glad y'all know it. If you run out of stuff to look at, I'll get you some more."

"Thanks, really. Thanks," said Stumpf. "And yes, I'd like to see if Leitner has been in any lawsuits in the past, say, five years. Either as plaintiff or defendant."

"No problem. Jerry? Anything?"

"Not for now. Thanks a lot, Connie."

Chapter One: Ramp up to today

Four years before David Leitner was found dead in his bed of an insulin overdose, two things happened. They were unrelated, but both were headed in the same direction, leading to their culminations at 36 Carriage Park Drive, where the Leitners lived.

It had been fourteen years since Leitner had gone bankrupt, the result of his trying to pay back money he had embezzled from the credit union where he worked. In a last-ditch effort to cover his tracks and avoid a criminal investigation, he had borrowed thirty thousand dollars from his neighbor, Clarence "Chip" Pullman, known locally as a small-time investor and day trader.

He was also known regionally as a lender of last resort, a "lender to friends in need," as he called it. Desperate friends, like Leitner. Even though Leitner had been paying on the loan for these fourteen years, he owed Pullman six hundred and eleven thousand dollars.

The other thing that happened was that Jean Leitner and Barry Cassidy had rekindled their affair. It was even more convenient for him, now that he was divorced. Jean had lost her virginity to Cassidy, and she was always there for another round, "for old times' sake." They both had feelings for each other, though Barry's were more carnal than amorous. Jean's emotions ran the opposite.

Jean only recently became aware of Barry's connection to Chip Pullman. Of course, she knew that Pullman had financed most of Barry's schooling and that he introduced him to various of his rich friends. She didn't know that Barry was the local one-man collection agency for Pullman's crooked loans, and she didn't know that her husband David was one of the debtors.

* * *

A year and a half before David's murder, Barry told Jean of her husband's big debt and his own part in trying to collect it. She was terrified to learn this of Cassidy, horrified that that her husband was carrying such a secret and huge amount of debt, and angry that he hadn't told her of it.

"Barry, you asshole! You little creep! You never told me you were working for a loan shark. I thought you were just a, you know, a successful lawyer. I'm as mad at you as I am with David. Over five hundred thousand dollars? That's impossible!"

"Really, Jean, really. I'm so sorry. I never could think of the right time to tell you. I didn't want to burden you. I…"

"The right time? Maybe before I married the son of a bitch! That would have been a good time, Barry."

"I'm just so, so sorry. I'm only bringing it up now, because…"

"Because why, Barry? Why now?"

"Because it's serious. Pullman wants his money. He's a neighbor, so he's not doing what he sometimes does, but…"

"Just what is that, Barry?" She was furious.

"Bad things. Really bad things." She calmed down. He continued. "Pullman wants David to step up the payments."

"Why doesn't he?"

"Your husband says he's strung out too far already. No cash. He's even thinking of selling the house."

"We don't have anything like half a million in equity. We could sell, but then we'd have nothing. We'd be homeless. *Nothing left*. He can't…"

"I know, Jean. So I told him I'd tell you, and maybe you could come up with an idea."

"Like what? Pull half a million out of my ass? If I could, I would. But it isn't there."

"Anything, Jean. Come up with anything, just to show him you're trying to help."

"Help some crook extort my husband?"

"No, make it possible for you to pay the loan back. A man with, say, a broken back, or even a few missing fingers, has a hard time doing that."

"You're serious."

"I told you I was serious. This is serious shit. Can you help?"

Jean looked out the window, then up at the ceiling, and found no answers there. She smiled at Barry, but he didn't return the smile. He just waited. "Maybe I could come up with a little," she said. "Like a thousand a month or something. Would that help?"

"Two thousand would. A week."

"Barry, that's crazy. How am I going to get that kind of money, week in and week out, without getting caught?"

"Good question, and you need an answer. First payment's due a week from Friday. Now, I gotta go."

* * *

Jean opened a new and serious topic after dinner that night. "David? Darling, I've been thinking. You know how you told me when we got married, that I'm, you know, so young, and

58

that my priorities will be changing as I grow, and you're, well, established. And you worried we might grow apart as I changed and you didn't?"

David was beyond surprised, and looked up abruptly, the look on his face indescribable. *Is she leaving me?*

"I just wonder, you know. What if I try so hard not to change, that you feel trapped being exactly as you were when we got married. I mean, what if you wanted a change of some sort, and I was holding you back?"

He sat up straight. Rigid, in fact. "Little Jean," using his most-intimate nickname for her, "What are you thinking?" He wasn't accusatory or defensive. More like vulnerable and open.

"I'm just saying, we've sorta been worrying about what if I 'grew' in some way, and then what if I wanted my life or our lives to take a new direction? I mean, I'm twenty-eight, almost -nine, and you're…"

"Fifty six."

"Right. And you always told me I'd be the one who would change. So I've been careful about where I let my mind go, what dreams I allowed myself. And I haven't even been thinking about, what if you wanted to change.

I'm worried that maybe I've been holding back your dreams. Have I? Can we talk about it?"

David stood up, walked around the room, stopped at the serving bar, the one that was always set up for company, but whose old drinks were never poured unless company was there. Jean liked liqueurs, maybe twice a year; David liked beer. But tonight, he opened the cabinet and took out a blue-tinted brandy glass and nearly filled it with V.S.O.P. "Want anything?"

"No. Sit down, love. Just sit down and talk to me. I'm worried."

"Oh, my baby," he said, as they both moved over to the sofa, "there's nothing to worry about. Whether you change or not, I'll always love you. I'm not too old to change, myself. As for dreams – I haven't thought much about them, and I'm sorry I haven't asked about yours. Must be painful. I'm so sorry."

"Lonelier more than painful," she said. "I mean, I've just figured you weren't going to change or dream or anything, so I was afraid to do it, and if I found I was doing it, I was afraid to tell you."

"So, tell me."

"What do you want us to be like when you retire? And when do you want to retire?"

60

David was still paying the mortgage. She knew that. He was also paying Cassidy on Pullman's ever-escalating loan. She knew that, too, but he didn't know she knew that, or so she thought. And she wouldn't have known, but for her continuing affair with Cassidy. And David didn't know about the affair, either. He struggled, torn between opening up and maybe losing her, appearing brave and in control, or taking some wishy-washy middle ground. Which is where he decided to stand. "I haven't given retirement much thought, actually. I like what I'm doing, and well, Social Security won't pay off the mortgage, you know."

"But when you retire? When, even *could* you retire?"

"I don't know. Like I said, I haven't even thought about it. Ten years, maybe? Maybe I'll just work a little less each year, and never actually give it up altogether."

"What would you do if we had the mortgage paid off, if you suddenly retired? I mean, we're not planning on having kids any more, like we fantasized about a few years ago. We don't need this big house, anyway. I mean, we could be free of all that…"

David's snifter, to his shock, was empty. He put it down on the end table, moved close to Jean, and put his arm around her shoulder. She moved closer. They kissed. He noticed her eyes were full of tears, though no drops had yet escaped. And she saw the same in his eyes. They stayed that way, together, silent…

"Let's talk," he finally said. "What are your dreams?"

"And I want to hear yours, too."

"You first."

She sniffed. "David, when we got married, I didn't hold out much hope for children. Your work was so intense, and you were…"

"So old." They both laughed, just a little.

"Well, maybe," she admitted. "I was envisioning you as an octogenarian, going to college football games and stuff, and I couldn't make it make sense. But me, too. I didn't have any great need to have kids. I don't understand, but I'm not all maternal, like that. "No, I was thinking maybe a simple, low-maintenance life. A small house a couple blocks from a beach – affordable, no tourists – and just, you know, laid back and enjoying life. In retirement, I mean."

"Ahhh, that's the life, all right. Where? San Diego, maybe?"

"I said affordable. It doesn't have to be in America, even. Marseilles, Cannes, Nice…"

"Monte Carlo, while you're at it?"

"Sure, but it doesn't have to be perfect, if you know what I mean. Georgia, Virginia, or – what the heck – Brazil, Bahamas, Chile… South Africa. They have nice places everywhere, right?"

"Jean, you mean, seriously, you wouldn't mind retiring out of the country?"

"Well, it's not like you've talked with anybody in your family for years, and, well, I'm technically an orphan, and an only child with no kids. Why not? I mean, what ties us to here at all, aside from your work?"

"True. I mean, brother Jim? I don't know if he's alive, in prison again, or what. He's older than I am, so, maybe… And Rick? I haven't heard from him since he went off on that 'quest around the world' thing with what's his name. That was two years ago."

"Three," she interrupted.

"Okay, three. And I guess, when you think about it, I'm an orphan, too." He chuckled. "Orphaned." He made it sound profound. "At fifty-six."

"So we're free to do anything, anything at all."

He perked up. "So, what would that be?" 63

$$* * *$$

Jean had planted the seeds of their escape, but she still had this problem of getting two thousand dollars a week to Barry Cassidy's boss. So she became a spendthrift, buying things she didn't need and showing them to David, who forgot about them and worked ever-harder to support her new habit.

She was convincing, convincing enough to get herself diagnosed as bipolar. It gave her a built-in excuse for being secretive, for "forgetting" things, for expanding her spending habit. David, sincerely in love and minimizing the problem in his own mind, just worked harder. Which gave her more time to raise money and conjure up schemes to hide it.

Jean went to out-of-town jewelers and bought expensive jewelry, which she showed David in her most-exuberant acting game. He'd figure out how to pay for it, even as she returned the pieces and pocketed the money. Sometimes, she'd just directly write a check to one of her girlfriends' shops; they'd cash her check, and the girlfriend would get a few percent. And sometimes, Jean would just withdraw a few hundred dollars, "to take the girls to lunch," she'd say.

David's insurance didn't cover mental health issues, and that was perfect, giving Jean another scheme. Her nurse friend got her receipts from a psychiatrist and a psychologist, again for just a few percent off the top. Jean paid for the drugs with cash, at a deep discount. And she sold those, too -- the good ones, anyway. David was beside himself. He didn't know she was saving his life. He thought she was killing him.

She was able to get two thousand dollars to Barry each week for nearly a year, even as she devised more and more radical excuses and behaviors. "I'm starting to think I really am crazy," she told her extortionist/lover. "And David's getting there, himself. I never knew that mental illness was contagious, but it is, even fake mental illness."

 "Cost of doing business," Cassidy always said, as David's debt slowly, inexorably grew.

* * *

It was in June of her last year that Jean couldn't handle it any more. She cut down on the payments to Barry, making little excuses that he knew were lies. When he reduced payments to Pullman and blamed Jean for absorbing David's payment money, the loan shark didn't fall for his made-up excuses for Leitner.

"You're running out of time with this particular client," he told him. "Come up with something."

They were sitting in her Lexus, outside the sandwich shop in the strip mall. It was comfy, as they had the windows partway open, and the mid-June breeze, under the shade from the lush greenery of the overhanging oak trees, protected the car from the direct glare of the sun.

It was Barry who floated the idea of having David's life insurance cover the debt. Jean was horrified. "He's… my husband!" she yelled into the collector's face. "And I love him!"

"You're running out of options, 'Little Jean,'" he said. She recoiled. She knew he knew more than he let on. *How?* All the years of friendship, all the years of love-making, the whole glorious, sordid affair – everything turned to dust in an instant.

"You bastard!" she screamed. "You asshole!"

Barry didn't flinch. He turned cold as stone. "This doesn't make your situation any better."

"*My* situation? How is this *my* situation? I'm trying to help here!"

"You're married to him. It's your problem, jointly and severally," the lawyer, the rejected lover said.

"We can't. We just can't any more." And she broke down. He reached over to her, and she snapped away. "Don't ever touch me again! Don't ever come near me again! Get out of my life!"

"I'm afraid you're stuck with me," Cassidy said. "Stuck with me until the end."

"The end of what?" Furious. Crying. Shaking.

"Until this debt gets paid off, one way or another. Because it will get paid off." As he got out of the car, he said, "You have until Wednesday to tell me your solution." He closed the door gently and walked away.

* * *

"What's the matter?" David could tell something out of the ordinary was wrong with his bipolar bride. She looked at him across the dinner table and started to cry.

As he watched her face for clues, she told him, between sobs, that she wasn't bipolar, that she knew all about the Pullman debt, that she had been faking an illness to funnel money to Cassidy. That she knew, that she was sorry, that they had to get together to fix it. And again, she was sorry. She got up from her chair, walked over to his, and knelt down next to him, crying uncontrollably, begging for forgiveness.

David pushed his chair back, and sat on the floor next to her, cradling her head in his chest, rocking back and forth on the dining room rug, sobbing with her. "I'm so sorry," he said. "I should never have gotten you into this. I should have told you, but I knew if I did, you would never marry me, and then, when you did, I was even more afraid you would leave me." And he cried quietly.

For long minutes, they rocked back and forth, holding each other, sobbing, and murmuring "I'm sorry" and versions of it.

"What are we going to do?" A broken man and a broken woman, two shattered people with not enough pieces between them to make one good soul.

"Little Jean?"

"Hmmm?"

"Let's get out of town. Sell the house, gather up as much money as we can, and go, somewhere. We can go anywhere. We talked about it, remember?

"Where?"

"Anywhere, anywhere else."

"Okay. Let's go."

* * *

Jean called Barry. "We can do it," she said. "We worked it out."

"Meet me at the sandwich shop in ten minutes," he said.

She detailed the plan to him: sell the house, pay off the debt, leave town. She didn't say to where.

"How soon will you be paying this off?"

"As soon as we sell the house. It's worth more than six hundred, for sure. That will get you paid off and give us a little to start over. We can do this, Barry. Just a few more weeks." She was too happy to beg. She was just telling him.

Barry looked back at her. He looked down, shook his head. "Oh Jean, Jean," he said. "You really don't get it, do you?"

"Get what? We'll pay you off. We'll pay everybody. Then we can be left alone, wherever we go. We can start over. In peace."

"Jean, you don't own that house. You have a mortgage. You sell that house for, for even seven hundred thousand, you'll only get three to keep. And you'll still owe Pullman five hundred thousand, plus interest. And don't even try to run away. We will find you. It's easy to find people, if you're motivated enough."

"Then… we'll never be out of debt?"

"Not this way. Look, there is only one way you can get it over with. I know it sounds hard, but I'm trying to save your future, maybe your life! Don't you understand that?"

She shuddered. "There is only one way to collect life insurance, don't you understand that? And I won't help you do it!"

"I'm not asking for your help. I'm telling you what you have to do. Honest to God, if you were anybody else, I wouldn't have stuck my neck out for you this far. You would already have collected that insurance money." He looked at her with cold eyes. "Both of you. I mean that."

She cried, looked down.

"Look at me." He didn't order her. He was acting like the lifelong friend again, the constant lover. "Look at me! This is the end game. There is only one source of money that will do it."

"David's life insurance is the only…?"
"Yes." He grabbed both her hands. She didn't pull away. Their eyes locked on each other, and this time his were warm, believable. Yes, even pleading. "Look, David got himself into this, before you even met him. He knew what he was getting into. He didn't pay on the agreed schedule, and he fell behind. None of

that was your fault. He didn't even tell you what he was getting you into. You tried to help, but you couldn't do it all.

"It's his mess, and he's out of time. He's going to go down for this, period. The only question is, are you going to go down with him?"

"I, I can't…" Looking down again. "Listen," hoping to divert him. Lying. "David told me he has a stash of money hidden in the house."

"How much? Where?"

"He didn't say, but I got the impression it was over a hundred thousand, maybe two. It's in the house. I could find it. It could buy us some more time, get Pullman off our backs…"

"Maybe, but he doesn't trust you any more. Look, it's a no-brainer. He's done, no matter what. You can't save him. Nobody can. You have a chance. Now, are you going to do the right thing, or what?"

She looked up, sniffed again. Not pretty, with her red teary eyes, her running nose, blotchy cheeks and wet stringy hair framing her face. She said, "Well, if I have to…"

"You do," Cassidy said softly, closing the deal.

"When? How much time do I have?"

"Two weeks. Less, if Pullman doesn't agree. But I think I can get you two weeks."

"Okay." She was barely audible. Then, "How do you want me to do it?"

"It's up to you, Jean. But he's a diabetic, right?"

"Yes. Type two."

"And you have syringes in the house, right?"

"Novo-something. Okay. Okay. Okay." She couldn't look at him anymore. "Two weeks?"

"Max."

"Okay." She sniffed again and went out to her Lexus.

At home, she counted the syringes in the fridge. There were exactly thirteen days' worth of insulin. *Perfect. We'll refill before they're gone, and there'll be plenty. Just an ordinary refill.* She broke down and sobbed herself into a fitful nap.

* * *

Two weeks later, her phone rang. It was Barry Cassidy. Jean picked up.

"Well?" said the familiar voice of the family lawyer.

"I'm going to. I am. We just got the prescription filled again yesterday. I swear I will."

"One day. You've got one day." And he hung up. It was Thursday.

* * *

Cassidy got on the phone with a guy he knew in Chicago. Same kind of business, a lawyer for a loan shark. Occasionally they did a little work for each other, when geography mattered. Adriano owed Barry a big one, anyway.

"Law offices," the receptionist said.

"Adriano Ippolito, please. Barry Cassidy here." She put him through.

"Well, Barry, how's it going? To what do I owe the honor? Or do I owe you money?" He laughed, an easy laugh from one friend to another.

"Hey, Adriano, remember when I took care of that trucking deal you had down here, and you said you owed me a big one?"

"No. No, I don't," said Ippolito, and he laughed again. "Okay, what do you need?" Barry told him, and included David's stash in the deal.

"So, Monday, unless you call me in the meantime. Carriage Park Drive. Thirty-six. Lexus in the driveway, left side. Got it. Say, is everything else good?"

"Thanks, Adriano. Monday, not before. And not after. Here's my burner number for your guys, just in case: 865-544-0751."

"Got it. Thanks. Monday, real early, before six for sure."

"'Bye."

* * *

Barry called Jean. "Tomorrow, right?" Her voice trembled as she said, "Tomorrow." She hung up.

* * *

It was Sunday night at the Leitner house, and Jean was downstairs. She tried watching television. She tried reading. She paced for hours, but she couldn't fall asleep. *I don't know how I got away with the weekend, but surely they won't give me any more time. It has to be tonight.*

She hardened her resolve. *Barry was right. Poor David, he's dead, no matter what. But I still have a life to live.* Jean walked to the refrigerator and took out a handful of insulin syringes. She went upstairs, where David was snoring loudly. *It's four in the morning. Why wouldn't he be snoring?* She pulled the cover off the needle and sank it into her husband. He didn't notice anything, just kept snoring. She repeated the injection. He sniffed and stopped snoring, but he didn't wake up. She did it again. He brushed at the needle, as if he were getting rid of a mosquito. Eleven times total, including four after David stopped breathing.

Jean walked back downstairs, trembling. She snapped the needles off in the 'sharps' box, dumped the syringes in the garbage, and sank into the sofa. She was trembling more, shaking so hard she was afraid that if she got off the couch, she'd collapse.

Then she heard the clicking, ticking of her back door's lock being picked, and the door opening. Two men were suddenly upon her in the living room, both wearing masks, one with a gun. The other one, very thick, she noticed, and carrying a duffel bag, put his finger to his lips, unnecessary because Jean was frozen in fear, unable to inhale.

The thick one walked up to her and put duct tape around her mouth, all the way around her head, her hair, everything. She could hardly breathe. Then he squeezed her nose, emphasizing her helplessness, as he handed the duffel to the gun guy and twisted her arm behind her. She could do nothing but look at him.

They explained that they would leave, and no one would get hurt, if she would lead them to the stash. "We're not going to hurt anybody," said the one with the gun, "but we're not leaving without it."

Then they tore the tape off her face, pulling a large amount of hair with it. "Now, where's his stash?"

Jean looked incredulous. "Stash?"

"Two hundred thousand dollars. We'll settle for one," the gun guy said, smirking. "Take us to it. We're not leaving without it." And the thick guy punched her brutally in the side. She felt, she heard her rib break.

Doubled over in pain, crying, Jean said, "What stash? There is no stash. I made that up! There's nothing here! But I am going to get the insurance! David's dead! I just killed him!"

"You shouldn't lie," said the thick one, and he punched her again. Another cracking sound, and sharp pain. "We came here to get the money tonight. Insurance? Not why we're here. Not our problem. We don't have months. We have – and he looked at an imaginary watch – two minutes. Now, get the stash."

"But it's not here!" she screamed. "There's nothing here! I made it all up!"
They dragged her upstairs, and shoved her into the guest room, a random pick. They didn't look

in the master bedroom, where David would never wake up. They started to push her through the guest room, into the guest bath. She broke free momentarily, and ran at the window, hoping to jump to safety, or maybe to her death. Then she tried, like a little child, to hide behind the curtains over the bed.

Recaptured, she was marched again into the bathroom and put in the tub. When she struggled, the gun guy slammed her head against the tub surround. She was delirious, but she could hear their repeated demands for the location of the stash. And all she could do was to repeat, through hysterical sobs and occasional screams, that there was no stash. But she was too weak and too afraid to move on her own.

The thick guy went back to David's room and retrieved a shoe, and put it on the edge of the tub, upside down. He didn't mention David when he came back. Maybe he thought David was sleeping. Maybe he didn't even see him. It was dark.

The gun guy grabbed her wrist and positioned her hand over the shoe's sole. Then Jean felt terror as the thick one pulled a meat cleaver out of the duffel bag. "Where's the money?" he roared.

She just looked at him, crying, hysterical, helpless. And he chopped off her fingers. Jean was trapped, watching her hand bleed, her fingers now in the tub, her hand on the shoe. "Where's the MONEY?" again. This time, the cleaver met her wrist, and she fainted.

"Bring her back," said the gun man, and the thick one slapped her face. Nothing. "Now!" shouted gun guy.

The thick man was frustrated. He grabbed Jean's other wrist, chopped again, but there was no response and little blood.

"Pain, you idiot. You don't want her dead before she comes to. Find that money!"

Thick guy pulled the pliers out of the duffel bag, grabbed Jean by the hair, wrenched her head back, grabbed a tooth with the pliers, and pulled. Jean opened her eyes, but did nothing else. Frustrated but encouraged, he pulled another tooth. Nothing. He pulled one more, and she again opened her eyes. They stayed open. "Where's the money?" gun guy roared again, but Jean was gone.

The thick guy went nuts. He pulled out all her teeth and got no response. Gun guy couldn't control him, and stopped trying when he saw the crazy look in his eyes, all that he could see through his mask.

As the thick guy continued to rage on Jean's lifeless body, gun guy called the burner number, said, "We're ready for a pickup," and hung up.

The bloody and mutilated corpse lay in the bathtub, with fingers, teeth, and hands alongside her, on top of her. Thick guy sat down. His rage was spent.

Gun guy apprised the situation. "Loco, we gotta clean this up and get out of here. Wash everything. Did you get any blood on you?" Surprisingly, very little. "Don't step in any. Wash her stuff off, and put 'em all in the duffel. And get every single part, every tooth, every finger, everything. Clean, we want it. And that fucking shoe. We don't want to drip blood all over the place."

All that was left of Jean was unrecognizable in the tub. Most of the blood was washed off.

"Here, get her onto this," gun guy Loverne said as he tore the plastic shower curtain liner off its hooks and laid it on the floor next to the tub. "Don't spill anything."

They picked up Little Jean and shook her over the tub, then set her on the plastic. They folded her body up and wrapped it in the liner, duct taped it in place so it wouldn't drip. Then they scrubbed up the tub, leaving nothing but water as evidence of their grisly deed.

Cassidy walked in through the open back door and closed it. He heard voices upstairs, and went up, announcing who he was. "David? Jean?"

"They're not home," said Loverne. "Did you bring our money?"

Barry was emotionally beyond his limits, thankful he couldn't see Jean's body clearly. He didn't know what horrors she had endured, and he didn't know that her hands, fingers, and teeth were in the duffel bag that sat on the bathroom floor, a duffel bag that also contained duct tape, pliers, a shoe, and a meat cleaver. He fumbled with the roll of cash he had brought. "Here," he said. "The rest when the body's gone."

"You're gonna help. Get a rug, or a blanket, or something to wrap this in," said Loverne. "And there is no stash. She woulda told us, for sure."

Barry nodded. He ran down the stairs and out to his car. He scrounged around and found an old blanket in the trunk, a blanket friends had abandoned a month earlier when they left an outdoor concert half an hour early, giving it to Barry and his date, who had walked over mid-concert and were invited to share it. "It's just an old blanket," said the missus, as they

left. "Just keep it." And Barry did, and it was
in this blanket that Jean's body, shower curtain
liner and all, was wrapped, then duct taped
and tied with rope the murder-for-hire pair
found in the Leitners' garage. The cinder
blocks came from the Leitners' back fence,
where a neighbor's dog, long departed, had
dug under it.

"Get the keys," said Lovrne to Barry. "I
think I saw them on the kitchen counter, er…
island. Whatever they call that."

Barry returned and popped open the trunk
on the Lexus. He tossed the keys to the two
hired thugs, who got into Jean's car. Barry
said, "Follow me."

Barry, trembling and heartsick, led them to the
Burger King parking lot, so close to the river.
When they wrestled the package out of the
trunk of Jean's Lexus, it was Barry who
dropped it, precipitating the cracked skull, if
the bathtub hadn't already done it. Barry
collapsed where he was, and the two thugs
dragged Jean's body far out into the river,
where the cinder blocks held it under four feet
of muddy water. Cassidy gave them the rest of
the payoff and they got into the Lexus and
drove off to pick up their other car. Barry
watched them go, turning left onto the street.

I owe Adriano a big one, all right. No stash. Jean is dead, can't collect the insurance. One big clusterfuck.

It was seven, and even though it was pre-dawn, the light was gathering quickly and the Burger King was open. Barry left the lot, hugging the perimeter lest there be video surveillance. He didn't care if the cameras, if they had any, had picked up Jean's car. It didn't matter now. *She lied to me about the stash, too, little bitch. Karma strikes again. She sure paid for that one.*

A few days later, a duffel bag containing body parts, pliers, a cleaver and a shoe, plus a dozen fist-sized smooth stones, fell from a boat on Lake Michigan, trailing bubbles for a hundred and fifty feet 'til it rested on the bottom, six miles from the Indiana shore.

Chapter Seven: Phony plate's a break

Two weeks went by, and Stumpf and Redding put a decent picture together for a progress report they were presenting to the chief and the other detectives.

Redding started. After some background, he explained where they were running down rabbit holes. "We know the Lexus was assembled and titled in Chicago, before it was sent to Atlanta. The Chicago salvage yard is under investigation. If they ID whoever brought it in, they'll tell us. Apparently they still do a lot of business there on a handshake, for cash."

Stumpf said, "We are working on the assumption that Jean Leitner killed her husband in his sleep with an overdose of insulin. The lack of any sign of struggle says he didn't wake up, and the sharps and syringes were found where they should be, not where an intruder would toss them." He added, "If I did it, I would have tossed them aside and gotten out of there, or, if I weren't wearing gloves, I'd have stuffed 'em in my pocket. So Jean's the probable killer."

"Why? Why did she kill him?" asked a fellow detective.

"In due time," Stumpf answered. "Now, Jean, she was literally torn apart. Pulled her teeth out, chopped her hands off... some of it while she was alive, maybe even conscious. We think somebody had a personal score to settle with Jean. But we don't know why it happened on the same day, or same night."

"And how do you know that for sure?"

"Because her Lexus was gone, and it never came back. And neighbors said it was there, for sure, the day before David's murder. Remember, we thought she had taken off in it." He looked around and added some police humor. "Well, maybe she did, but she wasn't driving."

Redding did a brief on the Leitners' finances. "David Leitner's laundromats were doing well. Very well. Much better than his books showed, well. But he didn't have any money, and he didn't show nearly enough expenses. Yeah, he didn't have any money. We didn't find any evidence of additional bank accounts, or any kind of stash.

"So David Leitner had off-book expenses. According to Barry Cassidy, his lawyer for the past two years and a long-time and ongoing lover of Jean Leitner at the time of her disappearance, David Leitner was devoted to his wife, didn't gamble. No one has come forward since his death with any significant claim against his estate; he didn't owe anybody a pile of money. But the fact remains that there's over a million dollars in the two years leading up to his death, that simply can't be accounted for."

Stumpf said, "So we're thinking extortion or blackmail, by person or persons unknown to us, but close to him. It's just that we have interviewed neighbors and a few friends, some people who managed his stores, all of Jean's friends that we could identify and interview, even his lawyer, her lover. And nobody has seen or heard of any evidence of any shady stuff going on. No midnight visits, no unexplained 'vacations'…"

The chief had held up his hand, stopping Stumpf. "So if nobody heard anything, saw anything, suspected anything, and you don't have anyone else to interview, then…" He looked to Redding to finish the sentence.

And he did. "Then we have already interviewed someone who knows what happened." He took a little bow.

The chief said, "So go interview them again, and start with that lawyer. He's close to the Leitners, real close to Jean. He certainly knows more than what you've told us he knows."

Stumpf made a motion to take over the imaginary mic. "So, we need ideas. What do we ask this lawyer, that won't spook him?"

The oldest detective in the room stood up. "Dig up everything you can on that lawyer first. Who are his other big clients? What do they do? How long has he been their attorney? Talk to his clients, the ones that will talk. The bigger the better. Don't worry about specifics – just get anything they'll give you. Then see what matches, what doesn't. Pretend you're a potential client. Ask if he ever got them out of a jam. And then find out who's claiming the insurance. Find those missing brothers."

Stumpf answered, by way of asking, "…and then do a second round of those helpful clients?"

"Right. And see if you can get Leitner's previous attorney to talk."

"He's deceased."

"Well, talk to his law firm, his friends who are still there, or even retired. This cuckold stinks. Sniff him out. He knows something." Another question came from the detective in the back corner. "Would the lawyer have anything to gain by having Jean dead? Maybe

he had his sights on Jean, rich insurance
widow and all, but what was the angle on
her?"

"And you said you'd tell us why Jean was
killing her dear husband. 'In due time,'
I believe you said." Here was the unanswerable
first question, again.

Stumpf took a breath. "Okay. If she were
alive, she'd get a million dollars life insurance,
net of all his problems, whatever they are. She
could pay off the house, and they didn't have
much unsecured debt – a couple grand, tops.
But dead? We don't think she figured *she'd* be
dead."

Redding summed up. "Well, we all have day
jobs, so we'll wrap it here. We're going to
make that second round of interviews, after
we talk with the old law firm, and after we
take a closer look at Cassidy's other clients.
Thanks for everything, guys. And if you think
of anything or find something out, well, let
Fred or me know. Thanks."

"Don't move until you're dismissed!" the
chief bellowed, and the six detectives
sheepishly took their seats. Redding and
Stumpf came back in from the hallway.
"Dismissed!" The chief laughed. "God, I love
doing that. Now get out of here."

* * *

Jerry and Fred went back to Fred's office. "Okay, Fred, what do we do, and which one of us does it?"

"Jerry, I'd like to talk with McGowan's old cronies at Erickson and Eckersoll. Maybe, too, there's a retired friend of McGowan's that would like to talk my ear off. Might take an hour, might take a long time to find 'em and get 'em talking."

"And I really don't like that smirky Barry Cassidy. Think I'll dig around, talk with his clients a little." Redding smacked the desk. "See you tomorrow. Call any time," and he stepped out, grabbed his sportcoat, and strode towards the door to the parking lot.

* * *

At ten the next morning, Fred and Jerry sat down in the cafeteria, empty since breakfast but with plenty of coffee fresh-brewed. "What have you got?" Jerry asked.

"Erickson and Eckersoll's reputation for stodginess is well-earned," he began, "and most of the lawyers who would talk with me — a total of two — didn't say much, but I chatted up their ancient receptionist, got her talking about the old days when Mel was there. Seems he was well-loved, and a character. Anyway, she told me the place hadn't been the same

88

without him, and then all the life went out when his best friend, Haskell Simon, left the firm a little over a year ago."

Redding's eyebrow went up. "You found Simon?"

"Yes, and he regaled me with tales of unwinnable cases, and clients he and McGowan used to trade back and forth, when the clients became too much trouble. 'They thought we worked as a team, rather than just fobbing them off on one another,' he told me. Apparently, they had two clients they both particularly hated, and they played hot potato with them for fifteen, twenty years, until one died four years ago, a year before McGowan died. McGowan was left holding the lousy client 'til he died, and the guy told me 'We frankly didn't want to keep him, so we didn't mind when that kid Cassidy thought he poached him from us.'"

"Who was it?"

"Chip Pullman."

"Chip Pullman, the investor?"

"Chip Pullman, the loan shark, more like. Ol' Chipster makes a lot more money off the books, with local cash loans, than he does through the front door."

"He told you that?"

"Well, first he offered me a drink. When I turned him down, he said, 'More for me,' and poured himself a *tumbler* of vodka on the rocks."

"Holy crap. And so how long were you there?"

"About an hour and a half. First we had to become friends, but he likes the Spartans…"

"The high school Spartans?"

"Yeah. He was a Spartan a hundred years ago, and they won the championship, you know, and I knew one of their old coaches, and all that. We talked Spartans for probably half an hour as he got lubricated."

"And he told you that Pullman has two faces? He's a very big deal in this town."

"Yeah, the richest. And he's loaned money to just about everybody who's anybody, and he somehow doesn't have his loans go bad on him, so he also has clout."

"And probably some really delicate legal problems."

"Those, too. And Mister Barry Cassidy, Esquire, handles all of it."

"And he handled Leitner's Whitie Tighties, too."

"You are sick, you know it? Yes. And Leitner. But you know what?"

Jerry took the bait. "No, what?"

"I can't find any other clients. Some walk-ins, you know, wills, prenups, divorces, maybe a small-time traffic violation if it's a friend's kid, but the only two sustaining clients he had, that I can find, were Leitner and Pullman. Now, just Pullman."

Stumpf waited for Redding to respond. He finally did. "You mean our man about town, with the fancy car, the expensive suits, the international vacations – he has only one client?"

"Now, yeah. Just Pullman."

"How much legal work does Pullman need?"

Stumpf said, "That's what I mean to find out."

"Mind if I help? I have an idea."

"Sure, Jerry. What are you up to?"

"Just keep doing what you're doing. You concentrate on Cassidy. I'm going to see if I can get a loan."

* * *

"Hi, kid brother. Got a minute?"

"Oh, shit, Jerry. Half-brother," said Charlie Redding. "What do you have for me now?"

Charlie Redding was nothing like his sixteen-year-older half brother. Unlike "Mr. Blackwell," he was often found in yesterday's

clothes, wearing a two-day beard and shoes
that needed shining three years ago, when they
had first worn out.

Charlie marched to a different drummer. To
no drummer, actually. He lived on odd jobs,
from framing carpenter to car mechanic to bus
driver, to IT professional, security expert,
white-hat hacker. He had a Private Investigator's
license that he almost never used. He seldom
had to call into play his old degree in
accounting, but he occasionally found it
useful, and, as he said, "It helps me stay
organized."

"Charlie, I need ten thousand dollars. And I
need you to borrow it for me."

"Good luck, Jerry. What kind of trouble are
you in, anyway?"

"Here's the deal. Police can't do what I need
to do, to find out what I need to find out. I
need a PI to find out how this guy works…"

After a five-minute explanation, Charlie
agreed. "Now, when do you need this
money?"

"Oh, whenever it's convenient for you, by
the end of this week."

"This week?"

"I'll bet you five bucks this guy does it," Jerry
said. "What we're trying to find out is how he

collaterizes his loans. Don't worry. You'll pay it back in time."

"Damn straight I will. Okay, give me the guy's contact info. And how did you say I got referred? David Leitner? What if he asks him?"

Jerry gave his brother the address and phone. "You haven't seen Leitner since last summer, and you've been out of town. You were only casual acquaintances, met at some art auction a couple years ago at the high school. Don't worry, Leitner won't rat you out. He's dead. Murdered. You didn't know."

"He's murdered? What – didn't pay his bill on time?" Charlie's chuckle at his own joke sounded hollow, even to him.

"Maybe. That's what we're trying to find out."

"Jerry, this could be real serious. You know what I charge for this kind of work?"

"Oops. Sorry, Charlie… you're breaking up. Hello? Hello? Can you hear me? Damn phone system!" Jerry hung up.

Chapter Eight: Charlie 'n Chip

While Stumpf tailed Cassidy, Charlie Newman worked with Jerry on his story. He needed to borrow ten thousand dollars, just for a week. He had the money wiring in, but it wouldn't clear in time, and he had an overdue debt he had to pay to some guys back home in Chicago.

Charlie came back here to his home town because he still had a few connections, one of whom, David Leitner, offhandedly mentioned that he could get him short-term financing for anything, any time.

By a lucky coincidence, Charlie had written the name – Pullman – on the inside cover of a book he had been carrying at the time. He rehearsed. "Am I talking to the right Pullman? If not, do you know the right Pullman for me to talk to?"

When Charlie prepared to make his approach to Pullman the next day, he admitted he was nervous. "That's good," said Jerry. "Makes you look like you're in a hurry for the money."

"Okay, wish me luck," he said to his big half-brother, as he dialed his 773-area cell phone and called Chip Pullman.

"Hello?"

"Hello, uh, Mister Pullman? Chip Pullman?"

"Who's asking?"

"Oh, this is Charlie Newman. I used to live there, er, here, but now I'm living in Chicago. I just came back this morning, because I wanted to talk with you."

"Do I know you? Why would you want to talk with me?"

"Uh, Mister Pullman, I was told a couple years ago that if I needed to borrow money, a lot of money on short notice, that you might have a way to finance a loan for me."

"Who told you that?"

"A guy I ran into a time or two, from here. David Leitner. You know him, right?"

"Charlie, is it?"

"Yes, sir."

"Charlie, have you talked with David about this, lately?"

"No, he's not really a friend, you see. We just met at the Spartan art auction a couple years ago, and I was carrying this book I was reading, and he mentioned your name, and I wrote your names into the book, because that was all I had to write on, and then I couldn't find the book, which book, and…"

"Slow down, Charlie. I don't need the whole story. So you got my number out of the phone book?"

"No, I Googled your name and your laundromat business came up. You're the right Pullman, aren't you?"

"Okay, Charlie. So, do you remember where the Starbuck's is, on Oak Street?"

"Uh, no. But I'm sure I could find it. Where, on Oak?"

"You must've left town a while ago. Oak and Central."

"Well, yes, I did. About ten years ago. But I get back every now and then. Oak and Central. When would it be convenient for you?"

"Give me forty-five minutes. See you at a quarter of eleven. Is that good for you?"

"I'll be there, Mister Pullman. Thank you."

* * *

"Hi, Jerry? He's going to meet me at a quarter to eleven, at the Starbucks, Oak and Central."

"Great, Charlie. Did he ask you how much you wanted to borrow?"

"No, as a matter of fact. Or what I needed it for."

"So, he's staying at arm's length until he sizes you up. Nervous?"

"Well, yes."

"Good. Now go talk to the man. And turn your GPS on, on your phone."

"I'm not getting less nervous here, Jerry."

"Get going."

* * *

Charlie arrived Starbucks at twenty to eleven. There were just a few people there. A pair of kids who looked like they were supposed to be in high school this time of day. An old bum-looking guy, slouched in the corner, browsing the web with the latest MacBook Pro. A grandmother, standing at the counter, making up her mind what to order.

Charlie saw a new Audi pull in and park. A tall, fifty-ish man with thick salt-and-pepper hair, in dress khakis and a white dress shirt, open at the collar, got out, carrying a black leather folder. When he walked in, he looked straight at Charlie.

"Charlie?" he asked, and held out his hand, which Charlie shook enthusiastically. "Chip Pullman. Can I get you a coffee? I haven't had mine yet this morning."

"Yeah, uh, thanks. Just a tall coffee of the day, black. Nothing fancy. Thanks."

"You already said thanks." Pullman smiled, toying with his new client's uneasiness. "Go sit down. I'll bring it over in a minute."

"Okay. Thanks," Charlie stammered, and picked the table farthest from the bum with the expensive Mac. He put a well-worn novel on the table.

Pullman sat to Charlie's side, not across the table, and he opened his folder. It had a blank yellow pad and a calculator.

"What's that?" Pullman asked, picking up the old book and thumbing through it, perhaps looking for a recorder. He put it back on the table.

"Oh," Charlie tried to laugh. "It's the book I had your name written in. Once I found it, I didn't want to lose it again." He showed his note: *David Leitner says loan from Chip Pullman OK*

Pullman was mollified. "I'm usually pretty informal about one-time loans," he said. "You're talking about just one shot, right – not long-term, complicated financing, right?"

"Right. I'll be able to pay you back in a week, tops."

"And how much money will you need for a week, tops?"

"I – I need ten thousand dollars."

"And when do you need this, Charlie... Charlie who?"

"Newman. Today, if possible. I have to pay a debt in Chicago, so I still have a four-hour drive ahead, so… right away, if possible?"

"Will you take a check?"

"Uhh, no. I don't think I can get it cashed. No offense, Mister Pullman. I just don't have an account here, and I don't have anything like that amount in my own account back home. I really need cash, if you can handle that much."

Pullman smiled, and Charlie wasn't supposed to notice, but he did. But he didn't let on that he did.

Charlie said, "So, you can loan me that much cash? Today?"

"Yes, if you qualify. First, let me see your driver's license." Pullman copied everything. "This your current address?"

"Yes."

"Your phone – the number you called me on. Is that your only phone, or is there another way to get ahold of you?"

"No, that's my only one. I always have it with me."

"Okay, we'll write it up. Ten thousand dollars, cash, loaned today. You say you'll have the money to pay me back by the end of the week?"

"Yes, for sure."

"Well, let's give you a little grace period, because it gets expensive if you miss the deadline. So, you can for sure pay me back by Monday then, right?"

"Oh, yes. That would be perfect. I'll still try to get it to you by Friday, though."

Pullman pushed his halfsie glasses up. "Try? I thought Friday was a slam-dunk."

"I'll try to get it to you Friday. Monday, for sure. I might have to do some important stuff in Chicago on Friday, over the weekend. But Monday for sure. Slam-dunk."

"Monday morning, by noon. Will that work for you?"

"Can we make it two? It's a long drive." Charlie was on thin ice. He wanted to see if he'd crack it.

"Two. Not a minute later. At my house."

"Where?"

"Where you're going to follow me, to get your money. But first, you'll need to sign this little note. It says you're going to repay me no later than two in the afternoon, one week from today, at my house."

"Oh," said Charlie. "And the vig?"

Pullman suddenly looked up, pushed back. "The *vig?* The interest? This isn't your first short-term loan, is it, Newman?"

Charlie stopped acting nervous. He was genuinely nervous, having betrayed himself. He recovered quickly. He flipped the book over. "Elmore Leonard, <u>Get Shorty.</u> It's about this guy who goes to Hollywood and gets some financing, and he says 'vig' when he means 'interest,' and…"

"Yeah, I've seen the movie. Get Shorty. Danny DeVito, John Travolta. Good movie. Anyway, the vig is twenty percent. Forty if you're a minute late."

"APR? How do we figure that?"

"A week, Charlie. Jee-sus. So next Monday, you're going to bring me twelve thousand dollars, cash. If I don't get twelve thousand by two o'clock Monday, it'll be fourteen. Problem?"

"No problem, Mister Pullman. I'll be there, on time. Twelve thousand. Thank you." Charlie signed, and Pullman snapped the folder shut.

"Now get in your car and follow," Pullman said. "And the coffee's on me."

"Thanks, Mister Pullman." Charlie mopped up the table and tossed the napkin in the trash on the way out. He had to rush to get into his car, as Pullman was a busy man, into his Audi, already.

At the house, Pullman walked Charlie into the living room, motioned to a loveseat, and said, "Wait here."

The living room wasn't large or ostentatious, but it was tasteful, in a sage green with glossy ivory trim, and nicely furnished. Early American furniture and some appropriate oil paintings on the wall. From where he sat, he could see part of what he thought was the dining room, a wistful beige, the same ivory trim somehow looking good there, too. Looking behind him, he guessed there was a hall, heading to a powder room and then the kitchen, but that was just a guess.

Chip Pullman returned, and he and Charlie counted out a hundred, hundred-dollar bills. Charlie folded the wad, stuffed it in his pocket. "Thanks again, Mister Pullman. I'll see you in a week."

"Or less," Pullman added. "But not more." And he nodded in the direction of the door. Business was done.

"Right," Charlie said, and as he closed the front door at the Pullman house, he said again, "Thanks, Mister Pullman."

* * *

When he was a block away from the Pullman house, Charlie called Jerry. "The guy's real," he said. "I got the ten grand, and I owe him twelve. Gotta pay him back before Monday at two."

"Good. Bring the money here, and we'll book everything in. Did you get a loan agreement?"

"Jerry, you nuts? He has the agreement. I remember it. It's simple – twelve grand by two on Monday, or it's fourteen after that. He doesn't mess around. He don't play."

Charlie and Jerry processed the cash and Charlie repeated the agreement, which Jerry transcribed carefully. Then Jerry turned his laptop around so Charlie could see the screen. "Is this Pullman?" he asked, as Charlie's jaw dropped.

"That's me!" Charlie said. "That bum in the Starbucks – he was recording the whole meeting! I knew something was funny about that guy, with that new MacBook Pro. It just didn't make sense."

"Yeah, we wanted to get a positive ID on the transaction. I'll have to tell Bobby to smudge up that new computer or something. He just got it last week. He's really proud of it."

"So, who followed us to Pullman's house, if you don't mind my asking?"

"A drone. Want to see the footage? We've got you leaving, too. Time-stamped. We rested the drone on Pullman's roof while you were in there."

"Jerry, you are an asshole."

"Yeah. Just looking out for ya, buddy."

"You're still an asshole."

"And you owe a loan shark twelve thousand bucks, and I have it. Be nice to me."

"Asshole."

"Sucker." And they hugged like the brothers they were.

Chapter Nine: Ronnie McGowan

"Hey, Tree, what have you got on our dear friend, Barry Cassidy, Esquire?"

"Jerry, the guy's a high-flying hermit. He goes to the bar every evening, goes home, sometimes with a honey, sometimes alone. When he goes home alone, his regular honey comes over to spend the night."

"Who's that?"

"Carlene. Carlene Gunther. Teaches school over at Saint Alexander's, sixth grade. Twenty-four, really short, maybe five-one, and, uh… stacked."

"Is she new since Jean Leitner, or did they overlap?"

"Haven't found out for sure, but from what I have found out, she's new, since January or so."

"What else?"

"Nothing. He's a weird guy. Goes to Jody's Place for breakfast, eats alone, then goes to his office in the strip mall every morning by nine. Has walk-ins until lunchtime, except Tuesdays and Wednesdays, when he goes to court, usually. After lunch, he's on the phone."

"How do you know that?"

"I call him sometimes. Other times, he leaves his blinds open. Well, open enough that I can see him pacing around with his phone, anyway. And once in a while, he goes out in the afternoon, but he's always back by five, when another guy – Ronnie, er, Ronald McGowan, stops by on those days."

"McGowan? As in Mel McGowan?"

"Yeah. Grandson, about twenty-two. Drives a beat-up Chevy, one of the little ones."

"Where does he drive it to?"

"Well, like I said, he only stops by on the days Cassidy goes out in the afternoons."

"So where does he go?"

"Oh, yeah. He goes from Cassidy's straight to Pullman's house. Goes right in the front door, stays about three minutes. Then he goes wherever."

"Wherever?"

"Anywhere. Home, to the store, to the bar. Just anywhere. Random."

"What else about Ronnie? Job? School? Background?"

"He graduated here. Played Spartan baseball. Ran errands for his grandfather in the old days."

"Old days – from a high school perspective," as Jerry rolled his eyes.

"Yeah, like when he was in high school, up 'til his grandfather died."

"Any other job? School?"

"No school. Took one or two night classes at Tech, still finding out which, maybe find a former teacher of his to talk with. Hasn't done any school for at least two years. He's been seen at Cassidy's place a lot, though."

"His place? His house?"

"No, office. Looks like he's running errands for Cassidy now."

"So, as far as you know, he has no job, hangs out all day, and sometimes, but not every day, drives from Cassidy's office to Pullman's house."

"Yeah, on the days when Cassidy isn't in the office in the afternoon. Two, three days a week. No pattern. And not every day that Cassidy goes out."

"Any idea where Cassidy goes?"

"Different places. Businesses, houses. Pretty much all over the place. Never stays more than four, five minutes. Maybe ten, once a week or so."

"So, Cassidy – let's start guessing here – goes around town, making collections, and when he scores, Ronnie takes the loot over to Pullman."

"And when he doesn't score, McGowan doesn't show up, 'cuz there's nothing to deliver. And most afternoons, he's on the phone, making deals. Or threats, maybe."

"Okay, Tree. So, where's our probable cause? How do we get a search warrant?"

"For what? Pullman's house, Cassidy's? Cassidy's office?"

"Yeah. All of 'em. Any of 'em. One of 'em – somewhere to start."

"How about we start with the little fish?" said Stumpf.

"You want him? Go get him."

* * *

Stumpf had a uniform in a squad car follow Ronnie McGowan on his next trip from Cassidy's. Two blocks from Pullman's house, the dirty Cruze rolled through a stop sign. Lights and siren.

McGowan pulled to the curb, opened the window halfway, shut off the engine, and put his hands on the wheel at ten and two o'clock. It looked like routine for the kid. Stumpf stayed back in his own car, unnoticed, lurking, listening to the officer's body-cam audio in real time.

License and registration checked out. "Where are you headed, McGowan?" asked the officer.

110

"Am I being arrested? Do I need a lawyer?" Ronnie wasn't being helpful. Well-briefed.

"Step out of the car, please," said the officer. "Slowly."

Ronnie complied. As the kid closed the door, the officer caught the shine of gunmetal blue between the seats. Ronnie walked toward the back of the car. "Please just stop right there, sir," the officer said. "Do you have a weapon in the car?"

"I'm licensed to carry, officer. My permit is right here," and he reached toward his back pocket. Or toward his backup gun, tucked into his belt behind him, maybe.

"On the ground! Hands behind you. Now!"

Ronnie said, "I have a license for that. I can show you."

"Show me later," said the uniform, as he put the cuffs on McGowan's skinny wrists. "Just stay right there and tell me where the gun is."

"Between the seats."

The officer put his foot on Ronnie's butt and pulled up the back of his shirt. Then he waved to Stumpf, who was on his way. Stumpf ignored Ronnie and searched the car. The gun was between the seats where the officer had already spotted it, where Ronnie said it was. Stumpf picked it up and as he was handing it to the patrolman, he "clumsily" knocked a paper bag onto the street. It split open, and a pile of cash fell out. Stumpf looked at the officer.

Then, for the first time, he acknowledged the young man, still on his belly on the pavement. "Lunch money?" he asked.

Ronnie said, "It's mine, er, I mean, it's not mine, but I didn't steal it. I'm delivering it."

Stumpf said, "Get up. Have a seat here." Ronnie sat on the driver's seat, feet on the door sill, hands still cuffed behind him. "Now tell me how much you have here, where you got it, and where you're delivering it to."

Ronnie said, "I want a lawyer." And he closed his eyes.

Stumpf said, "Okay. But we're going to count this right here, just to make sure everyone agrees how much." He counted slowly. "Five, twenty-five, thirty-five, thirty-six, forty-one, a hundred and forty-one…", and he stopped. "This is getting complicated." He made new stacks of each denomination, taking care that each bill was laid out perfectly flat, that all the bills were right-side up, with the pictures facing them. Ronnie was sweating profusely. The day was hot, and he was behind schedule, making his delivery to Pullman.

Pullman was punctual, and fanatical about it. Stumpf started over, slowly counting the hundreds first. There were forty-one hundreds when he stopped again. A ten was in the stack. He started to put it aside, into the pile of Hamiltons, when he slapped his forehead. "Oh, hell. I've lost count."

Ronnie said, impatiently, "Forty-one. There were forty-one hundreds in the stack."

Stumpf looked at the officer. "Do you agree? Forty-one?"

"Sorry," he said. "I wasn't paying attention. I got distracted. There's a guy in an Audi across the street. He's watching us."

Stumpf stuffed all the bills back into the remains of the paper bag, handed it to the patrolman, and said, "Watch this." And nodding toward Ronnie, "and watch him for me."

He walked over to the Audi, where Pullman was lowering his window, letting the air conditioning out. "Can I help you?" he asked the driver.

"No, er, I live in the neighborhood. I was passing by, and I was just wondering what was going on."

"Are you this man's lawyer?" and Stumpf pointed at Ronnie.

"No, officer, I…"

"Then move along, sir, or you will be
interfering with police work."

"Are you arresting him?" Pullman asked.

"Move along."

Back at the car, Ronnie was looking flushed.
Maybe it was the heat, but it was probably
Pullman.

Stumpf started the count again, first sorting,
flattening, and arranging the bills. When they
were finished counting, half an hour had gone
by, and the total was five thousand, two
hundred and ninety dollars.

"Everybody agree?" Stumpf asked. They
did, and he walked slowly back to his car to
get a plastic evidence bag and some paperwork.
He put the money in it, labeled it, and released
Ronnie's hands so he could sign the tag.
He quickly cuffed Ronnie again, made him sit
side-saddle as before. All three noticed as
Pullman went by, this time heading back the
other way, in the direction of his house.

"Well, young man, do you want to tell us
what you were doing with this gun and fifty-
three hundred dollars in cash in a paper bag?"
Stumpf was hot, too, and hungry, and thirsty.
And cranky.

Ronnie looked up.

Stumpf said, "Let's take him in. Maybe he'll be more talkative in the hole."

Ronnie said, "It's not my money. I was just delivering the bag to… somebody. I didn't know how much was in there. It's just my job."

Tree looked down at him. "And who's your boss? Was that your boss in the Audi?"

"No. That was… No. I work for a lawyer. I work for Barry Casssidy."

"So you deliver cash money for Barry Cassidy. Do you know where you were to deliver it? Or is that a secret, too?"

"I deliver to a house a couple blocks away."

"Where, exactly?"

"Up to the end of the street, left. Second house on the right. I don't know the number."

"Where that Audi is parked?"

Ronnie's face fell. "Yes."

"And how often do you deliver bags of money to that address?"

"This is my first time," Ronnie said.

"Might you change that statement if I showed you video of five more times you went to that house, in the past two weeks?"

"Oh, God. I need a lawyer," Ronnie said. "I'm not saying another thing."

"Fair enough," Stumpf said. He turned to the officer. "Take him in. Let's get this boy a lawyer."

Then he turned to Ronnie. "We'll take good care of your car. Mind if we search it, or will we need a warrant?"

"Search it. I don't care. Go… love yourself."

I hate Justin Bieber, Stumpf said to himself, as he walked back to his hot car and called for a police tow truck.

Chapter Ten: Only in horseshoes

Jerry Redding heard from Dr. Mills. "Hi, Jerry. I've got one more thing for you on Jean Leitner. Remember when I first said that the blow to the head could have been the cause of death?"

"Sure. But it's been blood loss for at least two months. What's up?"

"I've been looking at the x-rays again. There are two major hits, in just about the same place. That's why I couldn't figure the weapon. They occurred very close to each other in time, too, but I'm almost positive that the smoother one happened first."

"What's the significance of that? Does it change your ruling on COD?"

"No. She bled to death from that first wrist wound. She bled a little after that, but cutting off her hand is what killed her. By the time they got to the other hand, she was dead, for sure."

"What about the teeth?"

"Some before, some after, near as I can tell. I've never seen such rage."

"It's the sickest thing I've seen, ever, Hugh. Thanks for taking that second look."

"Welcome, Jerry. 'Bye."

* * *

It was Monday morning, and Jerry Redding
was surprised to see his brother waiting for
him when he came in. "Hi, Charlie," he said,
as he brushed and hung up his jacket. "Bright
and early, I see."

"Yeah, I don't want to be dead. I want to take
that guy his money." He returned Jerry's smile.
"You got my twelve grand?"

"You're kidding, right?" Jerry asked. "Hell,
no. You're not going to pay that crook. You
want to help with the case, right?"

Charlie turned bright red, then thought better
of what he was about to say. So he said, "Jerry.
This is a serious dude. I really meant to pay
him back on time, and I really have to, if you
know what I mean."

"I know what you mean, Charlie. But I don't
know what he's going to do when you miss the
deadline and you only give him half the
money."

"Half? That isn't even close enough for
horseshoes. I'm going to give him half, and
then walk away? "

"He won't get the other half if he stops you,"
Jerry said. "He'll know you're serious. We
have to know what his steps are."

"Steps? Before he pulls out my teeth?"

"Or cuts your hands off," Jerry said, reassuringly. He handed Charlie a bag. "Six thousand dollars. Nervous?"

"Fuck, Jerry. This guy'll kill me."

"No, he won't. You promise him you'll bring the rest tomorrow. Your wire didn't clear, and this is all you could scrounge up over the weekend. Tell him where you're staying, the Esquire Motel, and he can watch you if he wants."

"And so how do you get me the money tomorrow? In a squad car?"

"No, Charlie. We don't come for you. We come for him. Or we pay him off when you go to the bank tomorrow morning. Don't know yet. Depends on what happens."

"Jerry…"

"Don't worry so much. We got your back all the way."

"It's my damned back, Jerry. And my neck. And my teeth, and hands, and…"

"You're a guy. He might just cut your dick off."

"Fuck you, Jerry. I really mean it, fuck you." He grabbed the bag and started out the door.

"Perfect, Charlie. You're in the perfect mood to go see this guy. Don't forget to check into the Esquire. Room one-twelve is waiting for you."

"Fuck you, Jerry." He slammed the door on Jerry's jacket as he left.

* * *

Jerry had just sat down when Stumpf walked in. "Nothing more," he said, referring to Ronnie. "His lawyer – not Cassidy, some guy I don't even know – showed up, and he didn't say another word."

"Gun? Money?"

"Picked 'em up on the way out. Guess where he went?"

"Pullman's house?"

"No, Cassidy's office. No other clients in there at the time, as far as I could see. He went in with the bag, came out without it. In there about a minute, tops. Slammed the door on the way out."

"Then where?"

"Back to his own house. Maybe saw the tail. Maybe he just suspected. He made a point of stopping at each stop sign for about ten seconds, each."

"We're getting to him."

"Uh-huh." Redding grinned like a shark closing in on a surfer.

"Oh, guess what else? The lawyer for Jim, Rick, and Shane made an insurance claim."

"Who the hell are Jim, Rick, and Shane?" He stopped smiling, and Stumpf started, and Jerry continued, "David Leitner's long-lost brothers? …crap."

"Guess who the lawyer is."

"You're kidding... Cassidy?" Stumpf just smiled at Jerry's obvious angst.

* * *

It was a quarter before two, and Charlie Newman walked nervously to Chip Pullman's door. Before he could ring the bell, the door opened. "Well, you made it." Chip was all smiles. "You might turn out to be my best new client. Have a seat. Coffee?"

Charlie sat down. Pullman noticed he wasn't smiling. "What? Oh, for God's sake, you didn't fuck up already, did you?"

Charlie fidgeted momentarily, looking like a fourth-grader caught without his homework. Worse. "I didn't totally fuck up," he said, as he handed the bag with the six thousand to Pullman. "I… my wire didn't clear. I went all over town, borrowing. I got six thousand dollars, and…"

"Six? You owe me twelve, you puke. Six thousand? This isn't a fucking charity. This is no bank, where you can just walk in with some bullshit story, and expect to just walk out and start over. You came to me. I didn't go to you. You agreed. 'No problem,' you said. 'For sure,' you said. You lied to me. Now you sit here, in my house, and hand me half? Half?"

Charlie was crying. Genuine tears. He was scared to death, and Pullman recognized the true emotion. "Look," he said, in a calm voice. "I blew up. You did your best. You know it isn't good enough, don't you?"

Charlie nodded. And Pullman smashed a hard fist into the side of Charlie's head. He fell over onto the loveseat, sobbing. Pullman stood back a few feet, giving Charlie the space to recover.

"Here's how this works. You figure out how you're going to get me what you owe me, and I'll give you an extra day. You have until two o'clock on Wednesday, got it?"

Charlie nodded again, and winced, waiting to be struck again.

"You bring me fourteen thousand by two on Wednesday."

"Fourteen thousand? I just paid you six…"

And Pullman smashed him again. "I told you, and you agreed. Weren't you paying attention? If you didn't get me twelve by two o'clock today, you would owe me fourteen thousand dollars. Did you bring me twelve thousand dollars just now?"

"No, I..." and he winced, expecting another fist.

"I didn't hear you. Did you bring me twelve thousand dollars, yes or no?"

"No, I didn't. And I'm sorry, Mister Pullman, really, I'm…"

Wham, again. "What?"

"No."

"Okay, then you understand. You promised to bring me twelve thousand dollars by today, and you didn't, so you now you owe me fourteen thousand. And I even gave you an extra day. Isn't that fair?"

"Yes, sir, that's fair," Charlie managed to say.

"And don't try to run away. I have people all over Chicago. People who are not nice." Pullman walked out of the room, into the kitchen. Charlie heard the in-door ice cube dispenser. Chip came back with a washcloth in which he wrapped some ice. He handed it to Charlie, then stepped back. "Where are you staying while you're in town?"

"The Esquire Motel. It's on…"

"I know where it is. Now get your ass back to the Esquire Motel and get your mouth on the phone, and get that wire transfer in, so we don't have to go through this again." He rubbed his fist, as though it were sore.

"I might have to go to the bank, too," he whimpered.

"Do it if you have to. Now get out of here. I'll see you in forty-eight hours. Or less."

Stockholm Syndrome had already set in. "Yes, sir. Thank you, Mister Pullman."

* * *

Charlie's face swelled up until he couldn't see out of his left eye. He sat on the bed at the Esquire and called his half-brother. "Jerry, I just had a meeting with Pullman. Didn't go too well. He damn near killed me. Smashed my face concave."

"Man, I'm sorry. I didn't think he'd hurt you on a first offense."

"Well, he did. I think he broke my cheekbone, and I can't see, my face is so swollen."

"Feel terrible for you. So, how much time do you have?"

"Before he kills me or before I die of the injuries I've already got? Wednesday, two o'-clock. And now it's another fourteen thousand."

"Here's what I want you to do, and right now. Don't try to pack. Go out the back window -- we rigged it. You are in 112, right?"

"Yes."

124

"Good. Go out the back window. Take your wallet, phone, car keys. Leave the hotel key – you're not going back. Close the window; it will lock behind you. Go straight out the back, across that little bit of grass, down to the river. There's a path there. When you get to the path, turn right. Run, don't walk until you get to the Burger King. You'll see it up above you. Climb up the bank, stay in the leaves, hidden, until you see my car. I'll back into the corner of the lot. Passenger-side back door will be unlocked. Get in, don't slam the door. Doesn't have to close all the way, just latch. Get on the floor and stay there. I'll be in front. We may sit a while as I gulp down a Whopper. Hey, you want anything? I could order for you, too. On the house."

"I'm on the way right now. Yeah, get me a Whopper meal and a big ice water. Asshole."

Jerry barely had time to get his Whoppers and parked before he heard the back door open. "On the floor. Don't move until I tell you."

"Got it, asshole."

Jerry finished his meal in leisurely fashion, then put the car in gear and got on the main street. "Stay down!" he loud-whispered, when he heard Charlie start to move.

After he had traveled half a mile and assured himself that he wasn't being tailed, he said, "OK, sit up. Have a Whopper."

They went past the Esquire Motel, where three squad cars, lights on, a K-9 team, and six or seven uniformed officers were assembled, with one of the officers shouting something on a bullhorn.

"What the hell is that?" Charlie asked.

"They're picking you up. You're going to jail, isolation, protective custody. While they're doing that, you're coming to my house. We've gotta get you fixed up." He looked over the seatback at Charlie. "Man, you're a mess."

* * *

On Tuesday, Chip Pullman left the house, a suit and dress shirt hanging against the window behind him in the Audi. "He's going to be gone a while," Stumpf mentioned to Redding, as they sat in the unmarked, around the corner that Pullman never turned. "Tomorrow, anyway."

Redding said, "He's expecting Charlie tomorrow, with the money, but he should know that Charlie's been taken in, so he knows he has a little time. S'pose he's going to Chicago, to set up a hit on Charlie? It's Charlie's home, and Pullman told him he has 'plenty of people' there."

"You really got him into a jam, Jerry. How's he doing?"

"Got a helluva shiner, maybe a broken cheekbone. It's too sore for me to touch it right now. I messed up, got him in too deep. He's never done anything this dangerous before. I wanted him to be nervous, but he's about to stroke out. We gotta wrap this one up."

Chapter Eleven: Visiting the missus

Stumpf changed the mood. "You want to go visit the missus?"

"Let's," and Jerry started the car and then parked in Clarence and Vanessa's driveway. She opened the door, and Detective Redding introduced himself and his partner. "May we come in?"

"Of course, of course. I'm Vanessa Pullman. Chip's out of town, though. Is, is there anything I can do for you? Tea?"

They both nodded in assent.

Mrs. Pullman indicated the large sofa and invited them to have a seat. She repaired to the kitchen, and Stumpf laid his leather folder on the coffee table in front of him. The detectives looked at each other. Redding squinched his nose and Stumpf nodded. The sofa smelled like a cat had just had an accident on it. Or, being a cat, not an accident.

When she came back into the room, silver tea tray and elegant service atop it, she started at the sight of the folder. "Ma'am?" asked Stumpf.

"Oh, I thought Chip had left his folder," she explained. "He has one just like that."

Stumpf smiled and apologized. "Sorry for startling you, Missus Pullman. I assure you, I brought this one in with me. And thank you for the tea."

She took her own cup and saucer, adjusted the chemistry carefully with two cubes of sugar, and settled into the loveseat, as the detectives went through the motions of pouring their own tea.

"Missus Pullman," Redding began, "we're here because we're trying to help a young man. I understand you and your husband were longtime friends of a recently departed and well-respected attorney here in town, Melvin J. McGowan."

"Oh, Mel. He was like our favorite uncle to us, and he was a wonderful attorney, too. What young man?"

"His grandson, Ronnie. He seems to be running in a bad crowd. That hopped up car he has…"

"Oh, it's so loud," she interjected. "I wish he'd get that muffler fixed!"

"I'm afraid it's the way he likes, it, ma'am," Stumpf said, but Redding nudged his shoe and he shut up.

Redding took over. "Really, what we want to do is help young Ronnie. He doesn't seem to have a job, and…"

"Oh, but he does," she said. "I mean, it's Mister Pullman's business, but Ronnie works for my husband and his lawyer, Mister Cassidy. Ronnie delivers important court papers back and forth for them."

"Cassidy?" Stumpf asked, as though the name rang a bell.

"Yes, our new lawyer, since poor Melvin passed away. You know, I don't like his style very much. He's too flashy, or maybe he's just younger than I'm used to seeing in a lawyer, but Mister Pullman thinks the world of him, and I guess that's his department."

"Well, thank you, Missus Pullman. We didn't know he had a real job. I'm glad you and Mister Pullman are watching out for him. He's a good kid."

"Well, I hope so. He's always in such a hurry, though. Sometimes he's a little rude, I'm afraid."

"I bet you'll set him right, Missus Pullman. Thank you for putting our minds at ease. And thank you for the tea." They rose. Stumpf picked up his notebook, which he had never opened.

As he stood in the front doorway, Redding turned and handed her his card. "Thank you, ma'am. If you do think of something, please call me, any time at all."

"Have a good day, officers." She closed the door.

When they reached the car, Stumpf said, "Gawd, did you smell the cat?"

"Stop! Stop right there," Redding said, still holding the door open but not getting in. "And get me an evidence bag. One of the small ones."

Stumpf went to the back of the car, and after a moment of fumbling in the trunk, Stumpf handed him one. "What are you thinking?"

"Look at all these cat hairs on my suit. Let's get them into the bag."

"They won't hold up in court."

"Who cares? If they match what we found on the victim, we'll know we've got our guy. Narrows the field of suspects. Saves us some work, don't you think?"

"You know, it's odd for two detectives to show up in the middle of the day to ask about a dead friend's grandson's job."

"Yeah, I know that. But she didn't." For the first time in two weeks, they both smiled.

* * *

Stumpf walked the bag down to the lab. "Artie, you gotta help me, and quick. I need DNA on this hair, as much as you can find out."

Artie squinted at the hairs in the bag. "Don't know if you already know this, but this isn't human."

"It's cat. Housecat. And I'm hoping it matches the cat hair all over the blanket that wrapped up the Leitner woman."

"The one in the river?"

"The same."

"Well, Detective, I don't know how fast I can get DNA matched, but I can tell you that I can do a microscopic analysis really fast on the SEM… the scanning electron microscope. It's how they did this kind of thing in the '80s and before." *As if it's how the Egyptians did it.*

"How accurate is the match?"

"Could be proof positive. If it's not a match, I'll know that in a few minutes."

"Minutes?"

"Yes. As soon as I find the hairs from the blanket. Hey, you gotta sign this in. I'll get started on the other hairs."

Minutes. Why are we bothering with this DNA stuff? He attached the sheet to the bag and left it on the counter. "Thanks, Artie. Call me in minutes."

Redding heard Stumpf's phone ring a few times, then stop. Then his own phone rang. "Detective Redding, it's Artie. Detective Stumpf was in here a few minutes ago, and he sounded like in a hurry for what I could find out on these cat hairs. I just snuck his job in real fast."

"What do you want me to tell him?"

"One hundred percent, I'm sure."

"Sure they match, or sure they don't?"

"They match. I'm positive. I can explain…"

"No, Artie, save the explanation. I don't have time to understand right now. But you're sure, positive they're from the same cat. Right?"

"Yes, sir. Bet my life on it. Well, my cat's life."

"Good enough. Thanks, Artie. Don't bring lunch on Friday. I'm buying pizza."

"Thanks, Detective Redding."

Stumpf walked in, and said, "Jerry, I just dropped off today's cat hair at the lab, and Artie says he can…"

"Artie says it's a match, Tree. One hundred percent. Stake his own cat's life on it."

"How does he know?"

"I'm guessing here, but Artie's such a nerd and he likes his cat so much, I'd bet he's looked at more cat hairs than…"

"Than Missus Pullman?"

"Oh, God, Tree. I hate cats," Jerry said. "But I'm starting to love this stinky little snitch."

Chapter Twelve: Swiffer snitches

"Sorry to call you at work, Jerry, but since I'm going to die tomorrow, I thought I'd bust in on you a little by phone."

"Charlie," Jerry said, "I am really sorry what happened yesterday. We've…"

"Save it, Saint Francis. I just got a call from a new guy, reminding me I was living by the grace of God and his own patience."

"Who? New guy?"

"A new guy. Not Pullman. This guy said Pullman was out of town, and I could pay him, same terms."

"Charlie, why did you answer your phone? Was he calling from my number? Now everybody knows you're not in custody."

"He said he knew that, anyway. He was watching the window. Wanted to see what I did, while all the lousy actors put on the show out front of the Esquire."

"Did he have a name?"

"Yeah. It's Barry. Said what Pullman did was nerf tennis compared to what he's going to do, come two o'clock tomorrow. And he knows you and I are up to something."

"You mean because he saw the show, or because he followed you to my car?"

"Okay, Jer, this isn't funny. I really think this guy Barry is serious. He knows stuff. He's been watching your house."

"I wonder how long before Pullman's coming back in town, now that he knows what happened and what's up."

"My guess is that Pullman will stay out of town as long as I'm here, and let Barry kill me. And if I go back to Chicago, his Chi-gown guys will kill me. And when it's over, they'll kill you, too."

"You make it sound bleak, Charlie. To me, it sounds like we're making progress. Hey, stay put. I'm coming over to pick you up. And just for grins, go in my closet and put on my spare bulletproof vest. But don't worry. I'll be right there."

"Don't worry. Barry The Murdering Spy's probably outside, he knows I'm here, putting on the bulletproof vest. Don't worry. You know, it's been said before, but fuck you, Jerry."

"See you in five. Be ready."

"Got it."

* * *

Barry Cassidy was nowhere to be seen, and the ride back to the station was uneventful. On the way, as they both looked for a tail, Jerry apprised the situation. "You're still a mess, but half the size you were last night."

"And you're still 'fuck you.' So, what's the next plan, Sherlock? Set me on fire and throw me through Barry's window?"

"Better than that. We're going to arrest Missus Pullman."

"What? Missus Thurston J Howell the Third? What did she do?"

"Nothing. I don't think that dingbat knows what day it is, and she's as dangerous as a gerbil. But with her husband out of town, she's all the bait we've got."

"Bait? Arrest her? How you going to make that stick? You don't arrest bait."

"Just watch. You don't have anything else to do, from now on."

"Except stay alive."

"Right. Except stay alive."

* * *

As Charlie relaxed, if that was the word, in Jerry's office, Stumpf and Redding figured out how to get a warrant for Mrs. Pullman. "We can get a real one to pick up that stinky cat of hers," Stumpf said.

"It'll get us into the house again, anyway. And Mister Pullman's probably on his way back, maybe with muscle. We can haul him in for speeding, failing to signal a lane change, license plate light out… or something."

"You'd better, Jerry. When he comes down here to spring his wife, we'll tell him we just want to talk with him before we let her go."

"And if he says no?"

"If he says no, we'll tell him we're going to book his cat for the murder of Jean Leitner. Tell him we have his cat's hair on the blanket she was wrapped in. Maybe even show them both the blanket. See what she does, especially."

"She'll probably ask if she can have it back, to send to the cleaners."

"Meanwhile, Pullman's going to know we've got him. Does he want to talk with us, or does he want us to build a big ol' case and lock him up? Or just lock him up while we build a big ol' case?"

"Why don't we just build the big ol' case, lock him up, and call it a day?"

"Because he didn't kill Jean Leitner. He didn't chop off anybody's hands or pull anybody's teeth out while they were still alive."

Charlie piped up from the corner. "He tried to knock my teeth out. Does that count?"

"No, it doesn't, Charlie. Now, Fred, Pullman's a loan shark and he's a thug, but he's not a murderer. He has people who do that.

And little Barry is a weasel and a few other things, but he isn't a killer, either. He wouldn't do that to Jean, no matter how mad he got. Nobody would do that to somebody they knew, much less loved. Pullman and Cassidy are in on it, sure. They ordered the hit, or whatever they ordered. But that viciousness, that wasn't rational. That was animal. Rabid animal. And neither Cassidy nor Pullman is a rabid animal.

"So, we get a warrant for the cat. While we're there, we get Missus Pullman upset and offer to let her ride along with that stinky furball. Chip Pullman should be almost home by now. And he made it to Chicago, or he'd already be back. So he might have his muscle with him. Wouldn't that be lovely?"

Jerry slapped his hand on the table. "Let's get that warrant, and let's get that damned cat. Charlie, just stay here. Get a soda, or something. Just don't leave."

* * *

Mrs. Pullman was surprised to see the detectives again, and the animal team, and the warrant, but she was deferential and let them all inside. They quickly captured Swiffer, and put her in a transporter.

She grabbed Detective Stumpf's arm, pleading with him. "She hates those cat boxes."

"I'm sorry, Missus Pullman, we've gotta take her. But only for a while. It's just for some tests. We won't hurt her. Would you like to ride with us?"

"Oh, Swiffer would like that, I'm sure." The phone rang. Stumpf nodded for her to answer it.

"Oh, Chip, hello. It's so exciting here. The detectives that were here this morning?... Yes, they're back. They're taking Swiffer down to the police station... Right now, I guess. They're already leaving. Listen, Chip, I have to go. No, I can't wait fifteen minutes. I'll be at the station. Ta-taa, Doodles!"

Redding looked at Stumpf and mouthed, "Doodles." Stumpf nearly split a gut holding back his laugh.

* * *

A few minutes after Swiffer was in the proper hands, Chip Pullman and three other men walked into the station and demanded to see Mrs. Pullman. "Certainly, gentlemen," said the desk clerk, who walked around a corner and presumably contacted Vanessa, who presumably gave approval. The clerk soon reappeared at her desk, buzzed them through a steel door with wire mesh in the window, and said, "Please follow me."

Vanessa Pullman was in a small room, flanked by Detectives Redding and Stumpf. There was barely room for the four visitors to squeeze in, so Stumpf eased his way out, nodding to Pullman, who motioned for two of the men to leave. "Just wait in the hall," he said. Redding looked at the third man and Pullman said, "No, he stays."

Vanessa spoke first. "Oh, Chip," she said, as though they had all just sat down to tea, "I am so worried about Swiffer. They say she's maybe got something, a virus or something."

Chip Pullman looked at Detective Redding. "This is my attorney, Adriano Ippolito. I am here for you to release my wife."

Redding reached out with his right hand. "Mister Ippolito, I've heard your name before. Chicago, right? I didn't know you had a license to practice law here."

Ippolito looked at Pullman, then back to Redding. "In fact, detective, I don't. But…"

"But it's fine. She may leave any time. She asked if she could come here to the station. Missus Pullman isn't being detained. Swiffer Pullman is."

Ippolito looked puzzled. Looked at Chip, who said. "Swiffer's her cat."   143

Ippolito said, "I realize I can't practice law here, but may I just ask, out of curiosity, why Swiffer is being detained?"

Redding came to the point, looking straight at Mr. Clarence Pullman. "This is a criminal matter, Mister Pullman, and could become sensitive. And it's about you, not Missus Pullman. And counsel here isn't licensed in this state. Whom do you want to be in the room, while we chat a little about why Swiffer is here?"

"Adriano and I can handle it." He turned to Vanessa. "Honey, this could get complicated. See if they'll let you go see Swiffer, calm her down a little." And the room was comfortable again, with just the Chicago lawyer, Pullman, and the detective.

"Now, you're not practicing law here now, are you?" Redding asked Ippolito. "Do you know the law here? I mean, if you're not practicing law here, do you know if what we're about to get into is covered by attorney-client privilege?" He looked at Pullman. "Do you?"

Pullman fidgeted a bit and turned to the Chicagoan. "Would you mind?"

"You're the boss," said Ippolito, and the door closed as he left.

"Now, what is this all about?"

"I should start by saying that you're a suspect in a murder case." Redding made a circle in the air with his finger, and a red light on the wall-mounted camera came on. The detective Mirandized him.

"What's this about? I never killed anybody. Who's dead?"

"David and Jean Leitner, and specifically Jean, though we know David owed you a bunch of money and wasn't on time paying it back." Pullman's look told Redding his hunch was right. The detective didn't actually know Leitner owed him money, but… well, now he did.

"Leitner owed me some money. So what? He owed me money for years, but I never killed him. How would I collect? I mean, he was paying me, steady, but just not enough."

"A friendly loan, or with interest? I mean, if you were charging interest, the IRS should be able to back you up, and all."

"No, just a few grand. He was a friend of mine. I even recommended my lawyer to help him, when his old lawyer died. Been his lawyer a couple years. Worked out, I guess."

"So, he didn't owe you, like, tens of thousands of dollars, or anything like that?"

"Naw, nothing like that at all."

"Do you have him on your books anywhere? Any way we could confirm that?"

"Look, I said he was a friend. He wasn't on my books, which you need a warrant to look at anyway. I don't show my business records to just anybody who wants to see them."

"Okay, fair enough. Not necessary." Pullman was hungry. His wife and associates were out in the hall – or somewhere, maybe making statements to Stumpf. Or maybe just petting Swiffer, but the hunger made him want to get out and go home.

"Well, you said I was a suspect in a murder case, and it's not Leitner, so how can I help you?"

"It's not David Leitner. We have a suspect in that murder. You're a suspect in the murder of Jean Leitner."

"What? Are you nuts? I hardly knew her."

"Well, we figure either you killed her or your cat did."

"Okay, now I know you're nuts. Can I go?"

"Maybe you can help me out." Redding put a plastic bag on the table and slid out a nasty grey blanket. "That yours?"

"Damned if I know," Pullman said. "It's pretty wrecked."

"It's covered in Swiffer's hair, so we assumed it was yours. Can you help us out here?"

"No, really. Really, I can't. All that's Vanessa's department, anyway."

"Can we ask her, together? It would really help if we knew whose blanket this was."

"Hell, I don't care. I just want to get something to eat."

Redding leaned out into the hallway and talked to an officer. Back in, he closed the door, and he and Pullman stared at each other for a minute and a half. A knock on the door, and Vanessa walked in.

She looked at the disgraceful blanket on the table and recoiled a bit. Chip took the lead. "Honey, is that our blanket?"

"Oh, gracious, no. We would never have anything so awful."

"Uh, Missus Pullman," Jerry said, "did you used to have a blanket like this? I mean, was this your blanket?"

She looked at it and flipped a corner back and forth a couple times. "Well, I think this might have been ours, a long time ago, but the one I had, I gave it away. And it certainly didn't look like this."

Chip bumped her, to make her shut up, but Redding got to her brain first. "Just tell me about it, Missus Pullman. You're not a suspect, and whatever you say here doesn't count in court."

"Do you read me my rights, now, officer?" she asked.

"No, ma'am. We're just asking for your help."

"Well, the blanket we had that was this one, or just like this one, we gave it away at a concert last summer. It was almost worn out anyway, so Chip and I brought it to sit on. One of those 'symphony in the park' things, where everybody sits on the ground, like we're all hippies or something. I don't remember who did the music…"

"That's not important right now, Missus Pullman. Just tell us who you gave the blanket to."

She turned and looked up into Chip's puzzled face. "We left early, remember? To beat the traffic?"

Nothing from Chip.

"Anyway, our new lawyer, Barry, and his girlfriend, they were sitting with us for a while. They walked over after intermission, and we let them sit on the blanket. So when we left, I just told them to keep it."

Chip looked at Redding, but the detective was still looking at Mrs. Pullman. He asked her again, "So this was last summer?"

148

"Yes. I never thought I'd see that old thing again. And it looks terrible!"

"It does, doesn't it? Looks like it's been camping."

Chip asked, "So can we go?"

"Yes." He opened the door. "Thank you both. You've been such a help." As Chip brushed by, Redding said, *sotto voce*, "I'll see you tomorrow."

* * *

When Clarence Pullman opened his door to Stumpf and Redding, he was not jovial, but Mrs. Pullman, entering the foyer from the kitchen side of the living room, was ecstatic. Redding put the cat carrier on the floor, and she got on her knees to talk to her cat through the barred door. "Oh, Swiffer, welcome home! Did you get yummy tuna at the police station? Did you have fun with all the other kitty cats?" She opened the door, and Swiffer ran out of sight toward the dining room. "Oh, thank you, detectives. I…" and she looked at her husband, who looked like a weathered totem pole, and just as happy as one. "I'll make some tea. Or – I don't remember – did you like coffee?"

"Coffee, please," Fred Stumpf said. Redding nodded. Chip just glared. She hurried away. "This gonna take long?"

"Probably not. Just turn around." Pullman complied. "Place your hands behind your back." Redding kept talking as Stumpf put the cuffs on his plus-size wrists. "You are under arrest for the murder of Jean Leitner. You have the right to remain silent…." And the trio walked out the front door and got into the police car.

* * *

In the interrogation room, Chip Pullman demanded to have Barry Cassidy with him, before he would utter another syllable, though he did nod when they asked him if he wanted a Coke. "Yeah, diet. Thanks."

When Cassidy arrived, he made the usual inquiries about the arrest. Redding started. "Your client has been charged with the premeditated murder of Jean A. Leitner, and will be arraigned on Friday morning, Judge Markov's courtroom. We think he should stay with us, here in the jail, until arraignment."

Chip looked at his lawyer. "Get me out of here, Barry. I'm not staying two days in jail."

"No, you're not." He looked at the detectives. "You stay off him." And to Pullman, "and you, don't say anything. Not a word. I'll be back in an hour. Two, tops. You're going home today."

When the door closed behind him, Pullman disregarded his lawyer's instructions. "What are we going to do, just sit here until he gets back?"

"He won't get you released today," Stumpf said. "The judge already knows the circumstances of your case. He's just out saving his own neck."

Redding said, "We might as well get comfortable. May be a long wait."

"Comfortable? On these crappy steel folding chairs? With my wrists chained to this crappy steel table?"

"Oh, sorry," Stumpf said, from his padded and upholstered waiting-room chair. "I hadn't noticed."

Redding said, "Just on a personal note, I'm not happy how you beat up my kid brother. I think you overreacted a bit. Oh, I expected you'd add the fourteen to the six he already paid you, but I think the beating was uncalled for. So, I guess, bottom line, I don't care what kind of chair you're sitting in, until you get one with twenty thousand watts going through it. That's like, ten amps, two thousand volts of direct current, in case you're keeping score. You're good with math, right, Pullman?"

"Look, you sons of bitches. I didn't kill Leitner."

"We know. Your cat did." Stumpf laughed.

"Shut up. You heard my wife. She gave that blanket to Cassidy."

"Okay, so your lawyer killed her. The lawyer who was her lover for what – ten years? Sounds normal to me."

Redding stepped into the conversation. "Yeah, I'm always running around, looking for ways to kill my lifelong lovers, especially the hot ones."

"Shut up, you idiots. He didn't kill her, either."

"Want to venture a guess who did?"

"I'll *tell* you who did. And you already met them. Those two gumbos, were with me yesterday."

"The guys from Chicago?" Redding faked incredulity. "They looked like such nice guys. But if you say so… So why were they with you? Got more work for them?"

"I've said too much already. I'm done."

Redding looked at Stumpf. "I don't think he's done. I think he needs some more cooking."

Stumpf nodded, sagely. "More volts. Definitely."

"Listen. I know stuff. I haven't been an angel, but I didn't kill anybody. And listen, I'm sorry about your brother. I was having a bad day, real bad."

"Oh, then everything's okay, Chip," Redding said. "But what do you know, that can turn into some kind of deal that won't get you executed for murder, maybe even get you home for dinner?"

"I don't believe you. Either of you. Not one bit. I'm waiting for my lawyer."

"You think he's coming back? You think he doesn't know you, that you'd no way keep your mouth shut if you're innocent? He knows you're innocent, doesn't he? And how, exactly, would he know that?" Redding was relentless.

"Shit, you guys already know, don't you? About Barry's deal."

Redding looked at Stumpf, who took a chance, drawing two for an inside straight. "We have pretty good intel that says it was Barry who hired your friends from Chicago."

Redding kicked him under the table. *Are you nuts, Tree? You're completely fucking nuts. You just sent this guy home, with everything he knows, gone forever! Moron. I have a moron for a partner. Where's my Jim Beam?*

And Pullman smiled and said back to Stumpf, "That's some pretty good police work, Detective. So you do know I'm innocent. Then what's all this," and he rattled his chained wrists, "for?"

"You said you'd help us. Well, you're helping us."

"Then take these cuffs off and let me go home!"

"Can't. Gotta keep appearances 'til he gets back."

Chip relaxed. "Can I at least get a better chair?"

Redding switched chairs with him. "Okay, you already talked. Talk some more. We're listening."

"I want assurances."

Redding nodded to the door. Stumpf left. The two stared at each other.

"What's he doing?"

"Looking around for a bored District Attorney."

"What for?"

"To get you some assurances. I don't cut deals. But a DA can. Just sit tight."

It hadn't been three minutes when Stumpf walked back in, with a skinny twenty-some-thing-looking guy in a suit. "This is Assistant District Attorney Jacob Plessy," Stumpf said. "He's going to see what you've got that will keep us from putting you back in a different chair. We talked on the way back. What've you got for us?"

"In exchange for our not pursuing the death penalty, in other words, what can you give us that will lead to the prosecution of who you say is the real killer?"

"You're nuts. These guys," he looked at the detectives, "already told me they know I didn't kill Leitner."

"And you know who did. And that makes you just as guilty."

"Shit. So, since I said I'd help you, I'm guilty?"

"That's oversimplifying. But, well, yes, that's the gist of it."

"I don't think you'll convict me, because, as you know, I didn't do anything, but in exchange for the possibility of parole while I'm still young enough to appreciate it, I'll tell you the whole thing. Well, as much as I know, anyway."

Plessy stepped out of the room. He was back in half a minute.

"Thirty to life, no death penalty. Parole in fifteen. That is, if you give us enough to nail the killers and whoever brought them here."

"Twenty to life, no death. Parole in ten."

"Okay, talk. This better be good. No conviction, no deal. Understood? And before you answer that, you'd better get another lawyer.

Would you like me to get you a court-appointed attorney?"

"Better'n what I've got. Yeah."

Plessy turned to the detectives. "Just be patient. I'll be right back."

Redding replied. "When you come back, bring three chairs, OK? This one's no good, and you guys'll need to sit down."

Plessy left, and Stumpf stood up. There was a commotion in the hall. Cassidy was back. Stumpf went out, and a loud but unintelligible conversation tried to get through the door. When the door opened, Stumpf and Cassidy both came in. "Tell him," Stumpf said.

"You're fired, Barry. Get out."

"You can't fire me! We've got history together!"

Pullman looked up, smug. "Not any more. I've made my deal. Good-bye, Barry."

Stumpf closed the door behind the departing, fuming lawyer.

Plessy introduced everyone at the table to Pullman's new court-appointed lawyer, Cathy Ferguson.

Ferguson had attended law school with Plessy, the same age as he was but entered during the semester he graduated. Six feet tall and maybe a hundred and ten pounds, she looked too frail to stand up on her own, but her piercing brown eyes and jungle-thick long black hair, coiled in an enormous bun, made everything above her neck appear exotic, powerful, even dangerous.

Stumpf moved his chair to her side of the table, then talked with someone in the hall, and came back to stand in the corner. "They're bringing more chairs."

Plessy started. "Miss Ferguson, your client has said that he would like to exchange all his knowledge about this Leitner murder, for an assurance that he will not face the death penalty, and will face incarceration, if found guilty – he is not pleading guilty for now – of no more than twenty years to life. Would you like to consult with your client?"

Though Pullman said, "Yeah, do it," she asked that the others leave. Her knock on the door five minutes later again refilled the small room. "That arrangement is acceptable to my client," she said, "provided that none of what he says from this moment on will be used against him in this trial."

Redding and Stumpf conferred for a moment. Then Redding said something to Plessy. Plessy looked back at Stumpf, who nodded. "Agreed… We are recording this, of course, in audio and video, but I'd also like to say, Gentlemen, start your notebooks. Mister Pullman, you have our attention."

* * *

Clarence Pullman went after Barry Cassidy as if the lawyer had defiled his daughter. "He did most of my collections, especially my local ones. I didn't ask how, just gave him amounts owed, dates due, and contact information. If I knew something about somebody's habits or schedule or vacation, or that kind of thing, I gave him that, too.

"I never asked how he got the money, if he got it, which was nearly all the time. Once or twice a year, for one excuse or another, he couldn't collect."

"Example?" Stumpf asked.

"Well, this old guy owed me fifty, and…"

"Fifty thousand dollars, Mister Pullman?" asked Stumpf for clarity.

"Yes, fifty thousand dollars. He owed me that, and Barry came back with nothing. Said the guy had died. I checked, and sure enough, the bastard had died two days ago. But the way I figured it, he still owed me the fifty, right? So I suggested – I never told Barry how to do his business, only what had to get done – I suggested that Barry have a talk with his widow, see if he had any insurance.

158

"After a week – funeral and all, grieving widow, I'm not heartless – she didn't have any money, said there was no insurance. Damned if she didn't fall down an outside staircase at her condo, break a bunch of bones. She got out of intensive care – like I said, I don't want to bother people got no way to pay – and then, presto, there's the insurance money.

"Now, I don't know how much of that was Barry, and I don't know how much was just my good luck." He looked around the room. "Well, there's an example."

"Okay, well," Redding said as he leaned back from his notebook. "Let's get more specific on Jean Leitner. You said you knew the Chicago guys – you'll give us their names and whatever else you've got on them – the Chicago guys killed her. But how did they know her, and anyway, did she owe you money, or did her husband?"

"David. David owed me six hundred and eleven thousand dollars." Quick glances all around the table didn't stop Pullman. "He started a lot less, but he kept paying late, and every time he paid late, he'd owe me more, so it ran up to six hundred and eleven thousand dollars, by the time he was… by the time he died.

"I think Barry was probably skimming, but it didn't matter. If he did, it wasn't much, and it didn't grow, at least. It was pretty steady income for me."

Cathy Ferguson tapped his arm and whispered something to him. Chip continued, "Uhhh, on advice of my attorney, I retract that statement."

Plessy glanced at Cathy Ferguson. She shrugged.

Then to Pullman, "You mean about having loaned Leitner money?"

"No. More about the amount – the amount -- and stuff like that. I'd prefer not to get in trouble with the IRS."

Redding thought, *Here a guy's facing twenty to life, and he's more scared of the bloody IRS!*

"We'll pretend we didn't hear that, unless it becomes a key to the case. That work for you?"

Ferguson nodded. Chip picked up. "So David was paying me, but he was never going to start paying off the principal, and like I said, Barry was, you know, dating his wife. So I asked him if Leitner had any life insurance.

"Maybe the guy'll kick off or something. He's a diabetic, you know."

"Was," said Redding. "Continue."

"Yeah, was. And Barry tells me that she, Jean, says he's looking poorly lately, and she wants to stop making payments until he dies. Then she'll pay off everything."

Stumpf asked, "Did she say how much he was insured for?"

"Yeah, a million. So anyway, I say to Barry, no, just keep with the regular payments, same as always, and finish when he croaks. Next thing I know, they're both dead and nobody's getting the insurance money. Well, not me, anyway."

"So who are those Chicago guys, and how do they fit in?"

"Barry told me Jean kept coming up with one way after another that David didn't want to pay, and he asked me if I knew anybody who could, you know, maybe talk to him. I had my Chicago lawyer – you saw him, Adriano. I gave his number to Cassidy, see if he could help, maybe have some ideas. That's where the Chicago guys came from. Adriano recommended 'em, but Barry called 'em."

"And who pays them in a situation like this?"

"Like I say, as long as Barry sends me my steady, I don't get involved with his business."

Redding changed directions. "So, what do you know about what happened the day the Leitners died?"

"Nothing, really. I think the same thing everybody does. She was killing him, and somebody comes in to kill him, or both of them maybe, and they wind up killing her, 'cuz he's already dead."

"They?"

"He, they, she – I don't know. But I think she killed her husband, maybe to get the insurance. What I don't understand is why she stayed around. I mean why didn't she just take off with his stash?"

"His stash? How big was that?"

"Barry figured, he does the laundromat books, so he told me that Leitner was making a lot more than he was saying he made, and I sure was getting poor-mouthed all the time, so I couldn't raise my fee. And like I said, he was steady, and really, David was a nice guy. I liked him. So if he can't get ahead on his payments but he's paying steady, what am I to do?

"So Barry tells me he must have two hundred, two-fifty stashed someplace, 'cuz it's not showing up in his books, and I'm sure as hell not getting it, and he isn't spending it anywhere that Barry can find out, so… so it has to be going into a secret stash someplace."

"Didn't you want it?"

"Sure, but Barry said he denied it existed. So I figured they – the Leitners – were setting up a getaway fund, and they were probably getting set to disappear with it."

"Where do you suppose the stash is?"

"That's pretty hard to say. Barry couldn't find it, and he says he tried like hell to get it out of Jean, but she denied it, too. Said she didn't know what he was talking about."

"Did he believe her?"

"He told me he couldn't imagine she could keep that big a secret from him. I mean, he's known her since she was a teenager, and he's banging her, and she's told him everything else about everything. But he couldn't get a peep out of her about the stash."

"Maybe David didn't tell her?"

"What good would that do? I mean, if he's planning on running away? He adored her. Besides, if he thinks maybe he's getting too sick – he got that life insurance – why'd he do that, all of a sudden? If he's getting life insurance, and she's the beneficiary, why would he hold out on a couple hundred that she could just have, never have to tell anybody?"

"So, how does this make sense, then? David has a secret stash that he doesn't tell his wife about. He's skimming enough to make a pretty good pile, but he's not paying other bills, or buying stuff, or? Are you sure he had a stash?"

"So I take it you guys didn't find it, either."

"None of your business."

"So you didn't. No shame. Nobody else could find it, anyway."

Stumpf started a line of questioning. "How well do you know Barry Cassidy?"

"Known him since he was a kid. I found him in the newspaper, actually. Oldest of a mess of kids, single mom. I put him through high school, most of college. Then I loaned him money for law school, and he started working for me when he passed the bar exam. I'd introduce him to various people I thought could use a good lawyer. Introduced him to the Leitners…"

"After Mel McGowan died."

"Yeah, going on three years, now. Mel was a piece of work. Anyway, Leitner became Barry's largest client, 'cept for me. Reintroduced Jean to him, too. That part was probably a bad idea."

"Why?"

"Because he, well, he wasn't rational with her. Like he was still in love with her."

"Was he in love with her before?"

"Who knows? But he was goofy like that, when she got in the middle of stuff. He just was unpredictable. Not real rational, like he was with his other clients. Yeah, I'd say he was in love with her, until maybe six months before she disappeared. He stopped talking about her. But I knew he still saw her – she made the payments when David wasn't around, and he was working all the time. And that's why I still think he had a stash."

Stumpf broke in. "So, if we didn't find it and Barry couldn't get her to tell him where it was – or even if it existed, and Ippolito's boys didn't get it. God, they did awful things to that girl… And if Ippolito's boys couldn't get it out of her, where was the stash?"

Chip squirmed. "There isn't any stash, is there?"

"If there is, nobody's ever going to find it."

"So Barry lied to me about the stash?"

"I don't know. You say Leitner should have made enough to keep up with his payments, and let's say we think so, too. And there's no stash, and Jean's laundering maybe a couple grand a week herself – did we tell you that?

Oops. My bad – And Barry's handling all of the money,…"

"What do you mean? Jean's laundering two grand a week?"

"Sorry. I never said that." But his eyes gave him away, perhaps intentionally. Pullman saw it.

"That rotten son of a bitch. He was running his own racket on top of mine, and skimming from me and getting real money from Leitner and Missus Leitner, and making up all sorts of crap to tell me, while he's bleeding them dry. And now nobody's gonna get the million, and I'm never gonna get paid, and all because that little shit is running his own racket!"

"Are you done?" Redding asked.
Chip looked up, looking like he'd been punched in the gut. "How do we get him?"

"We find out how Jean Leitner died, and who did it."

"I hate the little prick, but it wasn't Cassidy." Stumph almost nodded agreement, but instead said, "But he was in on it. I still think Ippolito's boys did it. Maybe you could cut somebody a deal."

Plessy said, "We don't cut deals with murderers."

Chip looked straight at him. "But you cut one with me."

"Yes, but we knew you weren't the murderer."

Pullman turned deep red. "I'm getting twenty to life and you knew I didn't do it?"

"Well, you knew you didn't do it, too, and you took the deal. Now, do you want to fulfill your end of it?"

Chip said, "You let me talk to Ippolito?"

"If he'll talk to you, sure. We'll leave the room."

"But you'll be watching us, right? And recording?"

"Hey, it's our room, remember." Then he leaned out into the corridor and said, "See if that Chicago lawyer is out there, and if he wants to talk to our suspect. Alone."

Ippolito came in, and everyone left him alone with Chip, whose cuffs were still chained to the table.

"The fuck?" was the Chicagoan's less than cheerful greeting. "Why you want to talk to me?"

"Adriano, how long have you and I been friends?"

"Since… never?"

"Fair enough, but they've got hooks in me for the girl's murder, and I didn't do it, but I think Barry got your name involved."

"What's that creep got to do with anything?"

"Well, Adriano, he is in trouble. The blanket she was wrapped up in, it's got my cat's hairs all over it."

"So," said Ippolito, "You're in trouble."

"No, because they know Barry had the blanket last. Barry's in trouble, but he's going to have some excuse, or he'll just roll. He's been skimming from me, too, I just found out."

"You must have known that."

"Yeah, I figured a little here, a little there. But he was running a racket on top of my racket, free-riding. Maybe a quarter million bucks in the last two years."

"So, how do I give you Barry and not get in this, myself? What's in it for me?"

"Well, Adriano, you didn't kill her, either, right?"

"Right. And I don't know who did, really."

"Stop it. You sent two guys to find the stash. She didn't have a stash, or she didn't know. Really didn't know where it was. So your guys tortured her, pulled her teeth out. Cut her hands off, even."

"Oh, Christ. I didn't know that."

"That's 'cuz you weren't there. But your guys do, 'cuz they did her. Look, the sooner these morons get your guys, the sooner they'll get off our cases."

"Sorry, Chip. They're not on my case."

He said it as the door was opening. Stumpf walked in with two officers. "Yes, counselor, we are on your case. In fact, we're charging you with the murder of Jean A. Leitner."

"You can't do that," he said, making a half-hearted attempt to shrug off the officers who were putting the cuffs on him, as Stumpf informed him of his rights.

When he finished with Miranda, Stumpf made a point of looking at the camera, red light aglow. "You get that?" he asked, and he smiled at his two captives.

Redding took over now. "So, gentlemen, you are both charged with being complicit at least in the murder of Jean Leitner, and both of you are here because of the actions of one Barry Cassidy, whom we can't yet directly link to the murder, except that somehow his blanket," and he turned to Pullman, "your blanket, technically, the blanket was last known to have been in his possession."

Then he turned to Ippolito. "He called you just before the murder, and Jean's stolen car was recycled in Chicago a week later. We haven't exhausted all our leads with the chop shop, but we'd be happy to journey to the Windy City and have extensive talks with the owner, find out who delivered the car, who got paid for it, who their lawyer is…"

Ippolito opened his mouth, and Redding let him talk. "So everybody in this room hates Barry Cassidy, who is somewhere out there, laughing at us, with a quarter million dollars in his mattress. And we're in here, charged with a murder both of us and you guys" nodding at Redding and Stumpf "know we didn't commit. And the only way we can get out of here is to get him in here, and have him tell us how he set everything up. He probably set her up to kill him, too."

Redding looked at Plessy. "Have you filed the charges yet on these two?"

"No, not yet."

"What say we all walk out of here, like we just had a pizza party, and keep in touch?"

Plessy's look conveyed strong objection.

Redding kept up. "Look, if you haven't filed the charges, we can't keep these men here."

Then the ADA perked up. "But I could file them first thing in the morning, and you could pick them up again, and there wouldn't be any deals."

Cathy Ferguson, who had come back into the room same time as Ippolito, had been standing in the corner, silently watching her client help the prosecution. "Gentlemen, this is highly irregular. My client…"

"Your client hasn't yet been formally charged," Plessy said.

"But you…"

"But if you insist, I could charge him. Your call. Do you want me to charge him?"

Pullman looked at her. She said, "If he's not charged, he's going home. Now."

"Well, good night, gentlemen," said Redding. "Stay in touch. All these recordings get archived every five minutes, but no one's going to look at them unless we want them to. You make one move in any direction that screws with the case against Barry Cassidy and," and he looked toward Ippolito, "we'll rewind those tapes and share them around. Now Adriano, we'll see you at nine tomorrow morning, and you're going to bring your two boys with you."

He nodded assent. "And don't talk to them about anything." Another nod.

"And you," he turned to Pullman, "you need to find out where your lawyer friend is."

"Now, all of you, get out of here. Be back at nine in the morning, or we'll be on you like ticks on Pullman's cat."

They left.

Then he turned to Plessy. "So, can we get those wiretaps?"

"In five minutes, detective."

Chapter Thirteen: Chip's pizza party

"Hi, Barry. It's Chip. Call me. It's important." Chip Pullman, back at home in his living room with his new houseguest, turned to Adriano Ippolito. "I hate voicemail. But I think I hate lying, cheating, thieving lawyers more." He glanced at his friend. "You know I'm talking about that asshole, not you."

"Yeah, thanks. Good to keep your assholes straight. What're we going to do?"

"You're the lawyer. Got any ideas?" Ippolito said, "I think… better when I'm not hungry. Is there anything to eat around here?"

"Sandwich? Vanessa's out with the girls 'til probably nine o'clock."

"No. Let's go out. I'll buy." Then Chip's phone rang. He looked at it, then at Adriano, and said, "Barry." He answered. "Where the hell did you go?"

"Oh, sorry. Had to do some errands, and then a client showed up."

"In the afternoon?"

"Uhhh… yeah. Unusual, but I had to take him."

"Listen, Barry. This thing is closing in on us. We've got to talk. Can you come over? And what kind of pizza do you like?"

"So I'm not fired?"

"I just rehired you."

"A pizza party at Pullman's. I'll bring the beer. I got some Sands when I was in the Bahamas last month. It's cold."

"Okay, before it gets old. And what do you want on the pizza?

"Anything but anchovies or weird stuff. I'll be there in twenty minutes."

"Make it half an hour. I gotta order the pizza."

"Fair enough. See you in a little."

Pullman hung up and turned to Ippolito. "He'll be here in twenty minutes."

The Chicago lawyer nodded and dialed his own cell. "Loverne, can you get yourself and Loco over here in five minutes?... I'm at Pullman's. You know where it is… Great. See you. Oh – and park somewhere else."

Pullman looked at him with a question mark on his face. "They know where I live?"

"Uhhh, yeah. Just making sure I always have backup. They're staying at the Esquire, practically around the corner."

"Yeah, and a world away, too." Pullman ordered two Magnificent Sevens, giant thick-crust pizzas with seven kinds of toppings.

* * *

Loverne and Loco arrived, no car in sight. "What do you need, boss?" asked Loverne.

"Nothing just yet. We're gonna play it by ear. You guys ready for anything?" Nods. "Good. Loverne, go through there. Just wait in the little hallway by the powder room. Stay invisible. Loco, go out to the back door, real quiet. When you hear Barry come in, go around to the front door and wait right outside. He'll probably try to leave pretty fast, but you won't let him, will you?" Loco grinned. "So, go get by the back door."

And he headed for the kitchen, which opened to the back yard through a mud room. The pizza arrived, and the driver got a ten-dollar tip from Adriano. More like eleven and change, because Adriano didn't like to carry lots of spare change, and he had no use for one-dollar bills. The pizza guy said thanks, and as he walked out, he was pushed back inside by Loco.

"Oh, sorry, buddy," Ippolito said. "He's… uhhh… dyslexic. Please forgive us."

"No problem, sir. Thanks for the tip," he said, and the pizza guy got out of there.

"Okay, Loco. Same thing, but Barry this time. You remember Barry, from the other time you were down here, don't you?"

"Yeah. Different house, though."

"Right. Well, let's do it again. He'll be along any minute."

Loco saw the pizza boxes side-by-side on the table. The scent of their contents was unmistakable and irresistible. "Can I have some?" Loco asked.

"Sure. Take a slice. Just go." Loco removed one slice, folded it on itself, closed the box, and stacked the other box neatly on top. Then he headed out the back door, chomping on the pizza and remarking how it burned his mouth, but eating it anyway, to wait for Barry Cassidy's arrival.

Which was in two minutes.

Chip opened the door looking friendly. "Come on in, Barry. Yeah, pizza just got here. What's that beer?"

"It's made in the Bahamas. Sands. Good stuff. Try it."

"I'll go in the kitchen and get us some paper towels. Have a seat." Ippolito sat on the loveseat, opposite Barry, as Pullman went into the kitchen, got plates, paper towels, and a bottle opener, and told Loverne to stay alert along his way.

They opened the top pizza, and Chip spoke first, as everybody took a slice. "Barry, Adriano and I are on the edge of getting into some serious trouble over Jean Leitner. Seems the police – thanks again for abandoning us, by the way, Barry – the cops think we were involved in her untimely death. You know what happened to her, don't you?"

"Yeah, I heard. She died."

"She died, all right. Whoever killed her pulled out all her teeth, some while she was alive."

Barry's eyes opened wide and he looked straight into Pullman's. "Hell, no, I didn't know that. Holy…"

"And they chopped off both her hands. She bled to death."

"Oh, God, no!" Barry still didn't put the pizza down, though he sank into the sofa. "Oh, God. I – I didn't know. Really, I didn't… Oh, God."

"Yeah, and they think Adriano and I did it. And you know we didn't."

Barry didn't know what to say. So he told the truth in a question. He looked at Adriano and said, "Your guys did that? Your guys?"

Adriano grabbed another slice of pizza. "I believe so, but I wasn't there, and you were."

"You son of a bitch!" Barry yelled. "You know damn well I wasn't there. I didn't know. All I did was help your guys get her out of there. They killed her. I sure as hell didn't know what they did to her; I would never have let that happen. You know that."

Pullman grabbed another piece of pizza. "Look. Who did what – that's not it. We're all in this. Sure, they'll pick up the guys some day. Probably soon, right?" He looked at Ippolito, who nodded. Pullman had gulped down his pizza and went for another slice. Ippolito picked up his third. "But that won't get us off the hook. We need a story, and we need a plan. And we need it tonight."

Pullman sat down, finally, next to Ippolito. He looked at Cassidy. "First, though, Barry, I need some answers."

"About what? I wasn't there when it happened."

"Barry, this goes way back," Pullman said. He pushed the pizza box over to Barry. "Here, have the last piece and I'll get the box out of here. Think about what I might want to ask you while I'm gone." Pullman picked up the box and went into the kitchen as Barry and Adriano talked about beer and pizza. As he passed Loverne on the way, he mouthed, whispering to the tall hit man, "It won't be long. Make sure Loco is ready, but don't make a sound." Loverne nodded and headed to the

178

back door as Pullman re-entered the front room.

"So, Barry, I want some answers," Pullman continued. "The police told me Leitner was probably building up a stash, maybe to run and leave us behind. You know anything about a stash?"

"Well, I'm the one who told Mister Ippolito that he had one." He looked at Ippolito, who nodded in agreement. "But we didn't find it. So?"

"So, Barry, we didn't find it, and the police – I don't think they found it. So, where is the stash? Where did it go? His books – they're masking about a quarter million dollars that're just missing. And it looked, again to the police, like his faithful wife was setting aside money on her own, too. Maybe she wanted to run away from him. What do you think, Barry?"

"Well, I think they were both trying to hide money. Maybe Jean knew about David's stash. I couldn't imagine that if they were going to run, that she wouldn't be in on it. But Jean making her own?" Barry sat back in the sofa and finished the last bite of his pizza. He leaned forward, picked up his beer, and had another swig. Then he leaned back again.

Pullman said, "You're stalling, Barry."
Barry said, "No. I'm thinking. I don't really
know what to think, since nobody found either
stash, and your guys," he looked Ippolito's
way, "didn't get anything – nothing -- from
Jean."

"Well, I'll tell you what I think, Barry," said
Pullman. "I may be crazy here, but I think that
the cops are right about Leitner's books."

"How?"

"I think Leitner was making two, maybe
three hundred grand more than they're able to
find, but I don't think he was stashing it. I
don't think she was, either."

"What *do* you think?" Barry asked.

"I think," he said, as he opened the second
pizza box, "that I need another slice of pizza."

Barry looked at the second pizza. Before
Pullman grabbed his, there was already a
piece missing. But they hadn't yet started
when he got there. Barry thought fast. *No one
had any pizza when I got here. Chip even had
to get plates and paper towels. Then he had a
flash of panic. That means somebody else is
here! The cops? Oh, God – not...*

Barry jumped up and ran to the front door,
opened it, and ran straight into the arms of
Loco, as Loverne ran out from the hall by the

kitchen. The two dragged Barry back into the house and sat him down on the loveseat.

Pullman stood in front of Cassidy, as Loverne stood behind the loveseat, holding Cassidy down into the cushions, pressing down on his shoulders, and Loco stood between Cassidy and the door. Ippolito came around to the other side. Barry wasn't going anywhere.

Pullman continued. "Here's what I think. I think you weren't thinking too clearly when you used my blanket to wrap up your little dead whore. The blanket that brought the cops to my house. I think David Leitner was making his payments, even extra. I think Jean was making payments. To you. I think you skimmed off maybe – what are we all missing, two or three hundred? – three hundred thousand dollars. I think you stole from them.

"Worse than that, I think you stole from me. I think you scared Jean into killing her husband and counted on her to pay off the rest of David's loan. I think you set up Adriano here, just in case Jean did have a little set aside, something more that you could put in your pocket. But I think you didn't think too far ahead. I think you didn't think what would happen to my money, if Jean didn't get the insurance."

"I thought she'd turn over her own stash! I thought I could get you her getaway money."

"And you thought that would make me happy?"

"Well, yes. I mean, you'd get the getaway money while she waited for the insurance."

"Except, you crooked lawyer asshole shit, you already stole her getaway money, too."

Barry was looking up at Pullman. Ippolito shot a look at Loverne. Loverne let go Cassidy's shoulders, grabbed his head, and gave a violent twist. Barry Cassidy dropped his pizza.

"Get that garbage out of here," Pullman said. "And his car. And this time, get rid of the car. And not in Chicago. And don't sell it, for God's sake. Or at least destroy it first."

Ippolito said, "What he said. And I never want to see either one of you again. Get out of here. Now. And don't come back to Chicago. Go to… Cleveland. They'll be looking for you in Chicago 'cuz of Jean Leitner. Keep my car, too. And get rid of it. Keep the change. Just disappear for good."

* * *

Loco and Loverne dropped Barry's body into the trunk of their car. Which was really Ippolito's car. Loco followed Loverne in Barry's BMW.

182

"They're gone," Pullman said, looking out the window.

Ippolito made a call. "Hello, Detective Redding? Adriano Ippolito here. I'm at Chip Pullman's house, and I'm afraid I have a crime to report."

"You planning to come clean, or are you going to drop the dime on your partner?"

"Nothing that good, I'm afraid, Detective. Somebody stole my car."

"Aw, that's a shame, buddy. Call 911."

"No – I think I know who stole it, and where they're going."

"What are you up to, counsel?"

"My guys – Loco and Loverne – they're not at the Esquire, and they're not picking up my phone calls. We even tried using Chip's phone. They might have thrown their phones away, so they can't be tracked."

"How long have they been gone?"

"I don't know. I've only been at Chip's a few minutes. He looked out, at the driveway – and my car was gone. I have the keys, but Loverne drives me in it once in a while. He probably has a set."

"Okay, give me a description. You know your license plate? Give me their phone numbers, too."

Ippolito started with the phone numbers. Then the car. "Lincoln Town Car, two years old, real dark blue. Might look black, but it's dark blue metallic. Illinois license says B-L-O-M-E… Yeah, I told 'em I install foam-in-place insulation. Had some cards made and everything. They finally gave me the plate. Anyway, it'll make them easier to spot."

Redding said, "Just stay at Pullman's until I get there. I want to talk with you about a new development having to do with your lawyer."

"Cassidy? He's not my lawyer."

"Yeah. Your friend's lawyer. Meantime, I'll put out an APB on your 'blow-me' car."

"Detective?"

"Yes?"

"Loverne has family in Cleveland, and I don't think he'd come back to Chicago very soon, seeing as I live there, too."

"Thanks for that. Now, just wait where you are."

Jerry put out an urgent report on the car, either Illinois plate or, likelier, no plate, maybe heading toward Cleveland. Two occupants, probably armed, definitely dangerous.
He called Stumpf, who had gone home early. Well, only an hour late. "Hate to bother you, but the two Chicago guys are on the run. We'll

pick 'em up. Can you be right on it, when it happens?" Gave him the details. Then he went to Pullman's.

* * *

While Redding was heading to Chip Pullman's house, ostensibly to get more information on the car theft, Stumpf was making time on Interstate 90. About thirty miles west of Cleveland, Loverne and Loco were climbing into the Town Car on an on-ramp. Cassidy's BMW was out of gas and Loco abandoned it on the off-ramp just behind. Twenty-eight miles west of Cleveland, they were being arrested on suspicion of car theft. They sat, handcuffed, as Stumpf pulled up.

"Hello, Detective," said the State Police trooper. "They told me you were on the way, and just to wait, so here I am, just waiting. I've got a tow truck coming."

"Thank you, Sergeant. I can take 'em, unless you'd like to get them to our station."

"Let's get everything back to the post. I gotta get somebody else to sign off on giving these boys to you."

"Okay. Hey, let's give them a more-comfortable seat in the back of my car for now. You've checked them, took the keys, read them their rights? …They're not talking, are

185

they?" and the tall trooper smiled. "Good. Let's get them in my car. Have you searched the vehicle?"

"No. I just got 'em to this point, and you rolled up."

With Loverne and Loco locked in Stumpf's car, the detective grabbed his flashlight and walked over to the Town Car. Stumpf was banging on the flashlight. It was dead. "Hey, uh, Sergeant, you got a flashlight?"

The two met at the back of the car, and Stumpf hit the trunk release. As it opened, the flashlight immediately lit up Barry Cassidy's body. Stumpf looked at the sergeant and said, "I know this guy. We're gonna be here a while."

"Definitely going to the post first," the trooper added.

* * *

Redding's phone rang. "Excuse me, gentlemen," he said, and he stepped outside Pullman's house to take the call in private. "Who's in there? Oh, crap. Well, thanks. I'll wrap it up here. See if you can get anything out of the boys. I'll see you back at the station."

Back inside, Redding said. "So, you both think Barry Cassidy was collecting a lot more than was coming through to you?"

"Right," Pullman said, and Ippolito nodded.

"When did you get to that conclusion?"

"Well," Pullman said, "it just figured, especially after we talked with you. I mean, Leitner was making all this money, and I wasn't getting it, and nobody could find any stash. I mean, if there really is no stash, where would it have gone?"

"But why kill Jean? If she was willing to kill her husband to get the insurance money, and they were maybe planning to sell the house, well, there'd be plenty of money, right? With her dead, you'll never see that insurance. I mean, hypothetically, if that was your plan at all."

"Well, for the sake of argument, let's just assume you're right. Why would I?" and he turned to Ippolito, "and what would he, especially, get by killing her?"

"Makes no sense to me, either," Redding mumbled.

"So you know we didn't have anything to do with her death, then." Pullman was a little too quick, too self-assured.

"I don't know anything of the sort. I do know you, maybe him," motioning again to the silent Ippolito, "that you're a loan shark, a tax cheat, a crook, and not a very nice guy. But a killer? I never thought so."

The two suspects looked at each other, said nothing.

Redding took out his phone and said, "Give me a minute? I want to see if there's any news on your car."

"Hey, yeah. Me. Anything on that car yet? Okay, well, keep me posted. Meanwhile, can you send a squad over to Pullman's? Mister Ippolito's going to need a ride home," using their partners' code for "send a full, manned-up arrest team and as many warrants as you can get."

Redding had to stall a while. He addressed Ippolito. "Did you know either of the Leitners, yourself?"

"No. Never heard of them until this. Hey, I'm the *victim* here."

"Yeah. Your car's stolen. I know. I hope for your sake they are headed for Cleveland. Make them easier to find. No, I asked because I see you lived for some time in the Pacific Northwest, Bremerton, Washington, specifically."

"Yes, I did. Ten, twelve years ago, for two years. I needed some time off after my divorce, and I have family there. Why?"

"Well, I wondered about – do you know where San Juan Island is?"

"Yeah, just up from Seattle, in the channel. Almost Canada. Beautiful there. San Juan Islands. There's more than one."

"Do they have a beauty pageant there, Miss Island Tan?"

"Hell, I don't know. Not really my thing. But that would be a pretty stupid name for a beauty pageant."

"Why?" asked Redding. "Oh – and could I have a piece of pizza?"

"Uh, sure. Go ahead. Because it rains there all the time, and even if you got a decent day, it'd be too cold to get a tan, and there's trees everywhere, so even if you had sun, it wouldn't get to the ground. What's this got to do with my car?"

"Oh, nothing. It just fits into another case I'm working on."

"What's *that*?" Pullman jumped to his feet and looked out the window. Flashing lights on at least three cars were heading up his street. Redding quietly folded and slid his pizza slice into his jacket pocket, walked slowly to the window and looked out. "Looks like they found your car, Mister Ippolito."

Chapter Fourteen: Rolling

Detective Redding walked up to the Evidence Room's half-door and laid a ziplock bag on the sill. Artie came over, looked at it, and said, "Mmmm, pizza."

Redding smiled and said, "Don't eat it, Artie. Just log it under the Barry Cassidy murder case."

"Uhhh, Detective, we don't have a Cassidy murder case."

"You do now." Then Redding walked over to Dr. Mills's province of cold tile and stainless steel, where Barry Cassidy's body had just been delivered. "Hi, Quincy," he said.

"Your favorite people are dying too fast around here, Jerry. Can't you slow them down a little?"

"You know, for your sake, I'd like to. But for the broader benefit of humanity, I think this one is a net plus." He straightened his tie. "Can you get a good read on his last meal, Hugh? I think we can link that to our killer."

Dr. Mills was unbuttoning Cassidy's shirt. "I can get to that early, if it'll help."

"Yeah, thanks. And if it's pizza, save it. We may need to match it up to a sample I've got."

"Can do, Jerry. I'll let you know."

* * *

The next morning, Jerry had the email he was hoping for.

> Pizza, indeed. Three-meat. Barely
> digested, traces in windpipe.
> Indicates deceased may have been
> eating it when he died.
> COD is broken neck.
> —Mills

As he and Stumpf prepared for their debrief on the Leitner case, which now included Cassidy, he told Stumpf of his new evidence, and added, "Let's hope it matches the pizza in my pocket. Damn, I hate to do that to a good suit."

Stumpf asked, "How long you gotta preserve that suit jacket, before it goes to the cleaners?"

"I'm thinking never. I took it in this morning. It's the pizza we're trying to match. And it's going to match, I'm sure of it."

"Then we've got Pullman and Ippolito."

"And we'll have something that might turn Loverne and Loco. Where are they?"

"Down in lockup. Separated. They didn't say a word in the car, all the way here. Not even 'lawyer.'"

"How about the big guys?"

192

Stumpf said, "I looked in on them this morning. Same – separated and silent. Apparently, they're gonna get a lawyer in from Chicago, seeing as Pullman's local lawyer is deceased." They exchanged a fist bump and smiles.

* * *

After the debrief, in which Redding didn't mention the pizza, since he didn't have a positive match yet, Stumpf asked, "Who'd you want to start with?"

"Let's try Loco," Redding said. "He's crazy but he's a pro. He'll understand what we're building against him, and he may want to cut a deal. Who's his lawyer? Ferguson?"

"Yeah, she's got both of them," Stumpf said. "She's here, just waiting to see which of her clients we want to see, first."

"I'm going to get coffee. You want some?" Fred Stumpf nodded. "Okay, I'll see the three of you in the interrogation room."

* * *

When Detective Redding arrived with two coffees, Loco was already shackled to the table, next to Cathy Ferguson. She opened with, "Gentlemen, you are over-reacting to a vehicle theft."

Stumpf laughed a small laugh, and Redding noticed the corners of Loco's mouth turn upward, as the lead detective replied, "Counsel, your client may beat the car theft charge. He might claim he was kidnapped, or something. Or that he was sleeping in his boss's car when Loverne stole it. Or any old thing. But I think that there's enough evidence – oh, and Barry Cassidy's still-warm body in the trunk. I almost forgot – that he's likely to be getting free meals courtesy the fine people of this state, for the rest of his life."

Plessy walked in and said good morning to all. He took his seat and opened a file folder on his lap.

Loco looked at Ferguson, then at Plessy, but she said, "You have filed multiple charges against my client: the murder of Mister Cassidy, grand theft auto, being an accessory to the murder of Jean Leitner. What else are you planning to charge him with?"

Plessy said, "Nice try, Miss Ferguson. We may, in the course of our investigation, discover new charges. We may change some of the existing charges. For now, this is what you have to deal with. Now your client can help us or he can let us do all the work, in which case, we will be sure he pays handsomely for his lack of cooperation.

"What are you offering?"

"On which charge? What can you give us?"

"What have you got?"

"Positively, we have Loco here in a stolen car with a body in the trunk. The arresting trooper says he had pizza on his breath when he was apprehended, and Detective Stumpf confirms that."

"Eating pizza's not a crime."

"No, but it may be significant, since Loco's boss was serving pizza when he says his car was stolen. Anyway,…"

Ferguson's sharp glance didn't stop Loco from saying, "We didn't steal that car. He gave it to us. To Loverne."

Stumpf asked Loco, "Tell us more. If he gave you that car, why did you take the plates off? Where's the title?"

"I don't know. He gave it to Loverne."

"First it's 'us,' then it's 'Loverne.' Which is it?"

"Loverne. I was just riding along."

Redding asked, "Since you are both from Chicago, why were you headed the other way?"

"Mister Ippolito said he didn't want to see his car again. Told us to go to Cleveland."

"Do you have family there? Friends?"

Loco said, "No. I don't know nobody in Cleveland. Never been there."

"Does Loverne?"

"Not that I know of. Maybe. Don't know."

"So, why would Mister Ippolito give Loverne a car and tell him to take it to Cleveland?"

"Ask him, or ask Loverne."

Stumpf addressed Ferguson. "I'd like to ask your client how Barry Cassidy's body came to be in the trunk."

She said, "He doesn't know."

Loco nodded. "I didn't even know he was in there, until you found him," he added.

Redding went down another lane with his questioning. "So, Loco, what were you doing at Mister Pullman's house last night, er, evening?"

"We were having pizza."

"You and Loverne and Mister Pullman?"

"…and Mister Ippolito."

"And Ippolito is your boss?"

"Sometimes he has odd jobs for me to do. Cleaning up, driving, acting like a bodyguard. Anything where he just needs a guy around."

"Why were you there last night, at Pullman's?"

"I don't know. I guess he wanted Loverne and me to deliver his car."

"Does he do that often – give Loverne a Town Car and then have him deliver it?"

Cathy Ferguson broke in. "I believe my client has helped you all he can."

Plessy answered, "Perhaps." Then he opened the door and called for a guard to usher Loco back to his private cell. He turned back to Ferguson and said, "You might as well stick around. Loverne's on his way. Do you need a break? Could I get you some coffee? Soda?"

She mumbled, "I'll be back," and brushed past him, heading down the hall.

* * *

A cigarette later, plus two minutes, and Ferguson was back, taking her place at the table next to Loverne.

Detective Redding began. "So, Loverne, what were you doing in a stolen car with no plates and a body in the trunk?"

Ferguson broke in immediately. "My client wishes to invoke his right against self-incrimination guaranteed by the Fifth Amendment."

Redding didn't hesitate. "So, Loverne, what was *Loco* doing with you, in a stolen car with no plates and a body in the trunk?"

Loverne looked at his lawyer. She nodded. "Answer him, if you can."

"It wasn't stolen. Mister Ippolito gave it to Loco."

"Did he give Loco the title or a bill of sale?"

"I don't know."

"Why wasn't Loco driving?"

"Loco can't drive right now. He has too many points."

"So, Mister Ippolito gave his car to a guy who can't even drive? Okay, so why were you heading away from Chicago, when you live in Chicago?"

"Mister Ippolito's orders. He said to go to Cleveland, then he'd tell us what he wanted us to do."

"Did he ever tell you?"

"We never got to Cleveland. Your boys stopped us."

"Yeah, for not having a plate on the car. Why did you take the plate off the car?"

"Loco said to do that, since it wasn't Ippolito's car any more. Some kind of insurance law."

"Where is the plate?"

"I don't know. I gave it to Loco."

Stumpf took over the questioning. "Well, the plate, the stolen car, why you're heading away from where you work and live – that's all interesting. But what is more interesting is that body in the trunk. What was that doing there?"

"I didn't know he was there, not until you opened the trunk."

"He was still warm. Couldn't have been in there more than half an hour. How far a drive is it from Ippolito's, er, Pullman's house, to where you got stopped? Twenty minutes?"

"Who said I was at Pullman's house?"

"Okay, when and where did Mister Ippolito give Loco the car? Where did you get the pizza I smelled on your breath?"

"How could you smell pizza on my breath?"

"I was hungry. Sharpens the senses. Now answer the question. Where did you and Loco pick up the car?"

Loverne looked at Ferguson. She nodded.

"Okay, we picked up the car at Mister Pullman's. Mister Ippolito told us to get to Cleveland and wait for a call. I didn't know there was a body in the trunk. I just didn't look."

"How did you get to Pullman's?"

"In Mister Ippolito's Town Car."

"How did Ippolito get there?"

"I don't know. He was already there."

"Now, you and Loco are driving Ippolito's, er, Loco's car to Cleveland, but you don't know anybody there. This makes sense to you?"

"Look, officer,…"

"Detective."

"Look, Detective, I work for Mister Ippolito. When he says to drive his car somewhere, I just do what he says. It always works itself out."

"His car? What about driving Loco's car?"

"Aw, crap. You know what I mean. Mister Ippolito, he's the boss."

"Okay, Loverne. One last question, and I want a straight answer. Did Ippolito kill Barry Cassidy, and put his body in the trunk of Loco's car?"

Ferguson broke in. "Come on, Loverne. They can't ask you that." She turned to Plessy. "This interview is over."

They escorted Loverne back to his cell, and everyone else went back to their offices, silently going over their mental notes.

Chapter Fifteen: Too many murderers

Assistant District Attorney Plessy walked into Redding's cramped office, tapped Stumpf's open door on the way past, motioned for him to join them. "Gentlemen, we've got three murders, probably two dead murderers, and four suspects that we're going to have to release."

Redding looked up over the pile of papers on his desk. "You know we've got enough on Loverne and Loco. There's a dead body in their trunk. Ippolito's their boss, reported his car stolen so they'd get caught. And Cassidy was killed at Pullman's house, half an hour before we found him dead. And he was eating Pullman's pizza when he died. That sounds like a conspiracy in Cassidy's murder, at least. And Cassidy worked for Pullman, and it was Pullman's blanket that Jean Leitner's body was wrapped in. And Ronnie was delivering bags of money from Cassidy to Pullman. So who's going to release them, and when?"

Stumpf looked at Plessy, nodding his affirmation.

Plessy shook his head. "Here's our problem, gentlemen. There's three dead people. We're pretty sure who killed David, but Jean and

Cassidy? Which one of these four killed them? And, for that matter, did Cassidy kill her? How are you going to link anybody to any specific body?"

Stumpf looked at Redding, whose nod let him proceed. "So, we know these four are for sure related to the murder of Cassidy, and it doesn't take Detective Poirot to connect them to Jean Leitner. You're saying it's going to take a confession from at least one of them to make a case for murder, and we can't just hold them forever, right?"

"Not forever. Maybe one more day."

"What about on conspiracy?"

Plessy said, "That's not too bad. Not as heavy as murder, but we can charge them, maybe tag the Chicagoans as flight risks and get bail denied…"

Redding asked, "Can you keep all four of them locked up?"

"Probably, for a little while, at least. It'll be hard to keep Pullman. He's respected around here. Can you work with the three?"

"If that's what we get, that's what we'll work with," Redding said. "But it'd be better if you can give us some time with Pullman, first."

"You have a little time. Until about five o'clock. Then he walks."

"Well, let's get him in here." He raised his voice. "Tree, you coming?"

* * *

Cathy Ferguson was seated next to her client when the detectives walked in. Plessy was behind one-way glass, ready to listen to whatever was to happen.

"Where's the guy from McGowan's firm?" Redding asked.

"He's on vacation," Ferguson said. "I volunteered."

"That okay with you?" he asked Pullman, who shrugged.

"My client poses no risk," she began, "and he requests that the manacles be removed."

Redding played the advantage. "Leave them on. Your client needs to get used to them." Then he looked at Pullman. "The pizza in Barry Cassidy's stomach was a perfect match with the pizza you served him."

Pullman looked at his lawyer. She said, "So? How does that prove my client had anything to do with his death?"

"Aside from the obvious, Counsel, we also found the same pizza in his windpipe. That means he died while eating your client's pizza."

Pullman talked, obviously irritating his lawyer. "People choke on pizza all the time."

203

Redding replied, "But choking rarely breaks their neck. So, what we see is that Barry Cassidy died of a broken neck, in your house, eating your pizza. That puts you at the scene of the murder."

"I was in the bathroom. When I came out, he had left."

Redding looked at Stumpf and said, "This is getting better and better. He goes out to the bathroom and when he comes back in to see his guests, Cassidy, Loverne, and Loco have all left, and Ippolito doesn't know they're in his car, so he calls it in stolen."

Ferguson laid her hand on Pullman's, but he answered, anyway. "Right. Adriano was very upset. I didn't get it. Sounded strange to me, too."

"Do you have any idea why Mister Ippolito had this hunch that his stolen car might be heading to Cleveland?"

Pullman said with a cooperative air, "He knew one of his guys had family there, and he didn't think they would head back to Chicago. I mean, they wouldn't want him to find them, stolen car and all."

"And did anybody look for Cassidy's car?"

"We didn't think of that. We were thinking about the Town Car. Where was it, anyway?"

204

Redding stood, motioning for his partner to join him in the hall, where Plessy met them. Stumpf said, "It's not even close to believable. He's all over his story."

Redding looked at Plessy, and the ADA said, "He's not going to run anywhere. I'm going to let him go. We can pick him up later, if we have the case."

Redding and Stumpf looked at each other, and re-entered the room. "That's all for now, Mister Pullman," Redding said. "Thank you for your cooperation."

"We're done?" Pullman looked incredulously at his lawyer, as Stumpf unshackled him.

"For now," said Redding. "You understand we may have more questions for you as we get further into this investigation. You're not planning any trips, are you?"

"No. I'm here for good. You mean that's it?"

"You're free to go. Thank you for your cooperation. You understand our position, the handcuffs and all."

"I do, now," he said, as he rubbed his wrists. "Sorry I lost my cool. I'm not used to this sort of thing. Let me know if I can help."

"Oh, we will, Mister Pullman. We will." And then the room was empty.

* * *

"Hey, Tree," Redding called. "What say we have a chat with Mister Ippolito."

"What do you think, Jerry?" he answered. "Will he want Ferguson there?"

"Let's be easy on him. He's a lawyer; he probably thinks he can handle those 'gentle, cooperative' questions. If he asks for his lawyer, we can put him back on ice."

"Worth a try. I'll get him. See you in the room."

"And get Plessy behind the glass, if you can."

* * *

"Hello, Mister Ippolito," Redding began. "Thanks for being here."

"Screw you," the Chicago lawyer replied. "I heard Chip went home."

"Yes, that's true. He cooperated. You can go home, too."

"What do you mean, 'cooperated?'"

"Okay, are you ready to help us with this investigation, or not?"

"Go ahead. But if I want my lawyer…"

"You go back to your cell, and we'll get you one."

"I'll want my own lawyer, out of Chicago."

"Fine. Just make sure he's licensed here." Redding shot an over-acted wink at Stumpf. "Screw you. But what do you want to know?"

206

Stumpf asked the first question. "What were you all doing at Pullman's – Cassidy, Loverne, Loco, you?"

"We were having pizza."

"Great. Maybe you can help us with a couple lingering questions. Easy ones. Like, how did everybody get there? I mean, your car was there. Did you come with Loverne and Loco, or did they come in a different car? How did Barry Cassidy get there?"

"I don't know how Cassidy got there. I wasn't paying attention. Loverne drove me and Loco in my car. Before he stole it."

"Yeah, that's all fuzzy with me. He's your regular driver, and he takes off with Loco, in the middle of a pizza party, stealing your car in the process, and there's a body in the trunk. I mean, how did all that happen?"

"You want to know what I think?" Ippolito asked. Both detectives nodded. "I think they didn't like how Cassidy did business. Those guys know a snake when they smell one, and they've heard enough here and there to know he was skimming from Chip and probably playing the Leitners, too."

"So one of them killed him?"

"That's my guess. I went to the john. Indigestion. I was in there a while, if you know what I mean. Anyway, I got out and Chip says they all stepped out for a smoke. I think that's strange, since Loco doesn't smoke."

"Did Cassidy? Loverne?"

"I don't know about Cassidy. I never saw Loverne smoke; never came up. So, I go to the window to just look out, you know? Just curious. And my car is gone."

"What did Chip say?"

"Just, as I said, that they had all stepped out. He said he didn't hear my car start or anything. Didn't know they were gone."

"So then you called 911?"

"Right. And he," nodding to Redding, "came over. And you know the rest."

"What did you and Mister Pullman talk about, in the meantime?"

"Just, you know, 'What could have happened to them,' and 'Why'd they take my car?' That kind of thing."

Redding asked, "How did you know where they were going?"

"Well, I didn't, really. But I knew Loverne had people in Cleveland, or near Cleveland, at least. So I took a guess."

"And where did you think Cassidy went?" Blank stare. "I -- I didn't even think about him, actually. I was thinking about my car. Funny how you focus on one thing, and miss everything else."

"Didn't Mister Pullman wonder about Cassidy?"

"We didn't talk about it. Ask him."

"So, between the time you noticed your car was gone and the time I got there, and all through the time until you got arrested, you never wondered where Cassidy went? Nobody mentioned that Cassidy was no longer there, and you didn't know where he was?"

"Yeah, that must sound crazy. But, yes, that's right." Ippolito looked at the two detectives, looking in vain for a sign that they believed him.

Stumpf stepped back into the conversation. "So, you want us to believe that you were having a chance pizza party at Pullman's and went to the bathroom, and came back, and Mister Pullman told you that at least one guy you know doesn't smoke and two others went outside to smoke, and your trusted employees stole your car, and it had a body in the trunk, and you didn't notice Cassidy was gone at all, for at least twenty minutes, and Loverne was going to take your car to Cleveland?"

"Like I said, I know it sounds crazy, but…"

"You know that Loverne doesn't know

anybody in all of Ohio, don't you? We know that, so we know you're making at least that part of things up." He looked at Redding, who nodded. "Mister Ippolito, we're charging you with the murder of Barry Cassidy, conspiracy to commit said murder, making a false police report about your 'stolen' car, and lying to police in the course of an official investigation. We might have some more charges for you later, but for now, you're staying with us. You have the right to remain silent…"

"I want my lawyer," he said. "And not that skinny brunette. I want to make my phone call."

"Of course. We'll talk later. Thank you for your cooperation."

Plessy met Redding and Stumpf in the hall. "I'm taking you boys to lunch," he said.

* * *

"Anybody but me think it's ironic that we're having pizza?" asked Plessy, his suit jacket hanging on the wooden chair he was sitting in.

Redding said, "I've been craving pizza since I had to put my dinner in the evidence room."

Stumpf said, "Well, let's finish this pitcher of – what's this, Diet Pepsi? – and go back to the store and nail 'em."

And so they did. "You want Loco or Loverne next?" asked Fred.

* * *

Ten minutes later, Loco, a.k.a. Jesus Martillo, was waiting for them. Stumpf started the questioning. "Why 'Loco,' Loco? Why not 'Hammer' or something?"

"I want my lawyer," he replied, buying himself another few minutes.

Cathy Ferguson took her place next to him, and Stumpf repeated the question. "Go ahead and answer him," she said. Then she looked at Stumpf but said to Loco, "I'll tell you not to answer anything you shouldn't answer."

"My brother is 'Hammer,'" he began. "He's two years older than me, so I made my name by being the 'crazy' one."

"You don't have a Hispanic accent," observed the detective. "Why is that?"

"I'm second-generation American. Born and raised in L.A., Figueroa and Seventieth. Moved to Chicago six years ago. I don't even speak good Spanish."

"Please get to the point," said an irritated Ferguson.

"Loco, we've been talking to your boss, Mister Ippolito, and he says you don't drive. Is that true?"

"Right. I got too many points on my license."

"And he says Loverne drove him all the time. You just rode along. So, why does he need you?"

"I don't care why. He pays me. I do what he tells me to do."

"And what did he tell you to do at the pizza party at Chip Pullman's place, the night he says you and Loverne stole his car?"

"That's bull. He gave that car to Loverne. I saw him do it."

"And he told him to drive it to Cleveland? Why?"

"He didn't want us to go to Chicago. Said he didn't want to see us or his car ever again."

"Did he tell you to go to Cleveland, or just not to Chicago?"

"Cleveland. Said he'd give us instructions when we got there."

Redding broke in. "So, he set you up?"

"What do you mean?"

"Well, Loco, he sent you and Loverne to Cleveland and then called his car in stolen and told us where you'd be going. Doesn't that sound like a setup to you?"

Loco looked at his lawyer. She said, "Could we have a minute alone?"

* * *

When Stumpf and Redding came back in, Plessy was with them. The ADA said, "You want to go on the record? Come clean, be a witness?"

Ferguson answered for her client. "He wants full immunity."

Plessy answered, "In the case of The State versus Ippolito, I think we can do that. But we also need full cooperation."

"Draw it up," she said.

* * *

When the immunity agreement was signed, Loco told the whole story of the night at Pullman's pizza party, implicating Ippolito, Pullman, Loverne -- even Cassidy, in his own murder. He explained how Pullman and Ippolito were betrayed by Cassidy, how they had all surrounded him where he was sitting, how Loverne had killed him, even how he and Loverne had loaded the body into the trunk. By the time he was finished, he was exhausted and sweaty.

"Would you like a soda or something?" Stumpf asked.

"How about you take these cuffs off me?" he asked.

"No can do," the detective answered. Loco looked more puzzled than angry. "You have immunity in State versus Ippolito, but not all the other cases that are part of this. If it turns out you've told us the truth, you're off the hook for Cassidy's murder, but not for stealing the car."

"Whaaa? I told you, it wasn't stolen!"

"Then why'd you take the plates off it?" Loco just sat there, mouth open.

Ferguson said, "Just sit tight, Loco. That's bogus, and we'll prove it. You'll be out of here by morning."

* * *

"Loverne Washington, let me introduce myself. I'm Detective Jerry Redding, and this is my partner, Detective Fred Stumpf. We're here to inform you that you are being formally charged with the murder of Barry Cassidy, theft of the vehicle owned by Adriano Ippolito, obstruction of justice, and possibly some more things we'll get to, soon enough. You were already read your rights, and I see your lawyer, Miss Cathy Ferguson, is present. Let's get started, shall we?"

"I got nothin' to say," a sullen Loverne replied. "You can't prove nothing."

"Ah, but I can," said Redding. You were driving Mister Ippolito's stolen car, and Mister Cassidy's body was in the trunk. You were

214

heading away from your home in Chicago, and you had no plates on the car, no title, and no bill of sale. And you had a dead body in the trunk."

"You already said that."

"Oh, of course. Barry Cassidy's body. It's going to difficult for you to convince a jury you were just an innocent bystander in all of this."

Cathy Ferguson spoke on her client's behalf. "Mister Chip Pullman, a well-respected man in this town, has agreed to describe how my client was framed by Mister Ippolito. My client had no knowledge of anybody's body back there in the trunk, and he certainly didn't steal that car. It was given to him by Mister Ippolito. I'm having him – Mister Pullman -- wait downstairs right now."

"Okay, Mister Washington. Please explain just why Ippolito gave you that car, why he didn't give you a title or a bill of sale, why you were heading away from your home, to a city where you told us earlier that you knew no one, why you took the license plates off, why you were parked fifty feet from a dead man's stalled car, and – oh – why there was a body in the trunk, a body that was alive half an hour before you were stopped."

"He doesn't have to explain anything. It's your job to prove it," said Ferguson to Redding, while looking at Loverne, while placing her hand on his arm.

"Oh, we can," the detective replied. "We will. We already have your partner's testimony, along with statements from others. Of course, we also have you at the wheel of the stolen car, with the body in the trunk. It won't be hard. We're just looking for your cooperation, so we can maybe get you off with life instead of the death penalty."

"No more phony deals," said Ferguson to Redding. Then, turning to Loverne, she said, "They gave Loco immunity on the Cassidy murder, then they're charging him with car theft, anyway."

"Car theft? They're not charging him with what's-her-name's murder? -- chopping off that girl's hands?"

Ferguson squeezed Loverne's arm so hard it hurt. She looked at Redding, then at Stumpf. "I don't know what he's talking about," she said, "but he's not going to say another word."

Redding and Stumpf looked at each other, then back at Ferguson. "We'll see you both back here at ten tomorrow morning. Don't be late."

Loverne held his hands a couple inches above the table, as far as he could lift them against the chain. "Don't be late? I'm not gonna be late."

Redding turned to Stumpf. "Go get Pullman. He's talking voluntarily, so he doesn't need her. Just wait for me. Take them out the back way, first."

* * *

Redding was waiting in the conference room. It was larger and more-relaxing than the interrogation room, when Stumpf and Pullman entered. "Thank you, Chip. I didn't know we'd need your help so soon, but well, here we are again."

"Well," said an affable Pullman, "I do like this room better."

"Coffee? Soda?"

"Water, please. No ice."

"Don't worry. We don't have any ice." They both laughed as Redding held the chair for Pullman.

"You know Loverne Washington. He was at your house for the pizza, the night this all went bad."

"Sure. How can I help?"

"His attorney, Miss Ferguson, says that you will corroborate his story, that Mister Ippolito

217

gave him the Town Car. That he didn't steal it. They claim that Ippolito's the bad guy here, that he put Cassidy's body in the trunk, gave Loverne the car, then called in a phony 911 call to frame Loverne and maybe Loco for everything. What's your story?"

"Adriano's been a friend of mine for years. I really don't know what his game is. I don't know anything about why my lawyer's body was in the car. He stepped out with Loco and Loverne to have a cigarette, and…"

"Barry Cassidy smoked?"

"No. I think he went out with Ippolito's boys to see if they were up to something."

"Okay. So, Barry went out with the other two, and…?"

"I don't know, exactly. I went to the bathroom for a couple minutes, and when I came back into the living room, Ippolito was shaking Loverne's hand and saying, 'Enjoy the car. I'll see you later. Have a good trip.' He told me Barry had left for home and that he was sending Loverne on one last errand, and that he had given him the car as a going-away present. He had been shopping for a new car for a while, he told me."

"He didn't give anything to Loco?"

"I guess not. Didn't think about it at the time. Loco was still outside."

218

"Did Ippolito tell you how he planned to get back to his hotel, or back to Chicago?"

"No. Next thing I know, he's on the phone, calling his car in stolen, and telling them it's heading for Cleveland. Then you got there. I never got to talk to him about, well, about why he did that."

"And Barry Cassidy?"

"Like he said, Cassidy left on his own. I mean, that's what I believed, for about an hour and a half, until we all found out otherwise."

"Any idea how Cassidy got to your house?"

"I assume he drove."

"So where's his car?"

Pullman's affable demeanor changed to one of surprised truthfulness. "Right. It wasn't at my house… I have no idea."

* * *

Plessy picked up the phone. "Cathy?" he said, when Ferguson answered. "Hi. It's Jacob Plessy. Your Loverne dropped a bomb there, at the end of our little talk. How about you and your client work out something that tells us what he wants, so we can solve this Jean Leitner case?"

"You're offering a deal?"

"He's not swimming in options, Cathy. Everybody's talking. Everybody's going down.

The question is, how far down does Loverne want to go?"

"I didn't appreciate your last bullshit deal."

"No bull this time, and we can make it right with Loco. But look, you have two clients, both of whom could get death. Life might look better."

"Can I get back to you at ten? We're coming in then, anyway."

"That'll be good. But remember, we're trying to wrap up three murders here, Cassidy and both Leitners. We need something that'll close all of them."

"See you at ten, Jacob."

Chapter Sixteen: It was understood

Plessy, Redding, and Stumpf sat down for the critical strategy session.

Jacob Plessy started. "We have three murders – Cassidy, David, and Jean Leitner. They're all connected – all the same suspects, and one of them is already dead. But we know we have four guilty parties, and they all need real justice. Nobody walks, got it?"

"Whom could you convict right now, based on what we've already got?" Redding wanted to know.

"Nobody's a slam-dunk, as of right now, though we all know what happened, and pretty much who did what. To be sure of four convictions, we need solid confessions from Loco and Loverne. Ippolito and Pullman aren't likely to roll; we're going to have to sink them, ourselves. Or get them to sink each other. Or get Loco and Loverne's credibility up."

Stumpf said, "Tell me if I'm getting any of this wrong. Pullman's a loan shark. Cassidy collected for Pullman, who loaned money to maybe both Leitners, who didn't pay, er… pay enough. Maybe they did, and Cassidy was just putting it in his pocket.

"Anyway, Pullman got impatient with Leitner. He didn't know Cassidy was skimming, so he told Cassidy to put the pressure on. Cassidy put the bug in Pullman's ear that the Leitners were going to skip town, with some stash he made up, probably about equal to how much he'd been stealing from Pullman, but Cassidy still had an affair going, maybe even had feelings for Jean Leitner.

Redding interrupted. "You know," he said, "I just had a thought. Pullman never gave us any hint that he was impatient with Leitner. Do you think Cassidy…"

"Do I think that creep made up Pullman's 'impatience' so he could put more in his pocket? Well, now that you mention it, yeah, sure.

"But let's go on. Leitner – David Leitner – has a million-dollar life insurance policy, and Cassidy convinces – or scares -- Jean enough to kill him and collect it, but she delays and delays.

"So Pullman calls Ippolito and has Barry work out the details. Ippolito sends down Loverne and Loco to collect the stash, but they get here too late to get it from David, because Jean has finally killed him. But their job is to collect the stash, and since there isn't any stash, they escalate, and they – one or the other, sounds like Loco – kills her.

"Then they clean up and wrap her body in the shower curtain and call Cassidy, 'cuz they didn't figure on it going this far. Cassidy comes over and grabs the blanket from his trunk – the blanket Missus Pullman gave him at the concert, with the cat hair on it – and they wrap up Jean and dump her in the river, and Loco and Loverne go home, stealing Jean's Lexus in the deal.

"Are we good on that part?"

"Plausible."

Redding said, "So at this point both Leitners are dead, Loverne and Loco are back in Chicago, and they're getting rid of the Lexus, probably without telling Ippolito. Just a couple of entrepreneurs, selling a stolen car…

"But Pullman is pissed at Cassidy for stopping his income stream. He snoops around a little and figures out that Cassidy has been skimming and that there never was any stash. Now he didn't get the stash, he owes Ippolito, and Cassidy has betrayed him. He tells Ippolito, who's also ticked off that he's been led on a wild goose chase. And so they figure out how to get rid of Cassidy, Loco, and Loverne all at once. That's where the pizza party comes in.

"Ippolito has his boys kill Cassidy and sends them to Cleveland, calls and reports the car stolen. It's an easy stop. No plate. Body's in the trunk, still warm. Loco and Loverne go down. Ippolito and Pullman don't have bloodstains on their hands. They both seem to have gone to the bathroom at just the right time."

Plessy said, "So we've got Loco and Loverne. Do you want Pullman and Ippolito? What've got on them?"

"You're the guy who can indict a ham sandwich. What do you need to convict it?" Stumpf asked. "Loco and Loverne – one of them, either one – could put Ippolito away, and I think we can get both to do it. What do you need to get Pullman?"

Redding said, "I want Pullman more than anybody. It's my fault he beat up my brother. I've got to make it up to him." He looked down, hesitated. Then, softly, "Got to. He hates me now, and I understand why. My brother, I mean. On the other hand, Pullman thinks I'm his buddy."

Plessy looked at both detectives. "We've got the blanket. We've got the pizza party, but to get him for the murder, or the murders, you're going to need Ippolito to turn on Pullman.

Maybe letting Pullman -- and everybody else, especially Ippolito -- think he's getting away with all of it…?"

"Ippolito's already mad at Pullman," said Stumpf.

"Yes, let's let him think it's Pullman sold him out," added Redding. "That should send him over the top. So, I'll send Pullman home?"

"With a tail," Stumpf said. Redding and Plessy nodded.

* * *

Cathy Ferguson sat with Loverne in the interrogation room, as Redding came in. Plessy was behind the glass. Microphones were hot and cameras were rolling.

"Good morning, Miss Ferguson," Detective Redding began. "You understand this is your client's one and only chance to make a deal that will spare his life."

Loverne looked at her, pleadingly. She said, "Yes, and my client is prepared to cooperate fully, in return for the ironclad promise that he is not to face the death penalty in any of the cases – Cassidy or either Leitner. And no extradition to anyplace else. And no more trials in this state, either."

Redding nodded. "You understand?" he asked Loverne, directly.

"Yes, sir."

"All right, then. We're good with that. Tell me everything about your trip to the Leitner house last September."

Loverne Washington spilled every detail, from the moment he was told to drive Loco to the Leitner house, to not leave without the stash, to his surprised horror at how seriously Loco had taken that order. He told of Cassidy, how the lawyer didn't know Jean Leitner's hands, fingers, and teeth were in his duffel bag, how they didn't remember seeing David Leitner. He told about the Burger King parking lot, Cassidy's breakdown, and how he and Loco decided to steal the Lexus and sell it in Chicago.

Ferguson and Redding let him talk without interrupting. Loverne finished and asked if they had any questions. Ferguson was silent.

Redding asked, "Where are her teeth, her hands? Where is the duffel bag?"

"At the bottom of Lake Michigan, somewhere," Loverne said. "They're in the bag with a bunch of rocks."

"Could you lead us to where?"

"I doubt it. I really didn't take a good look around. I just dropped it over the side."

"Why was there so little blood?"

"Loco an' me, we're professionals," Loverne said. "We had plenty of time to wait for Mister Cassidy. And we didn't want blood on ourselves, either. So we did a pretty good job of cleaning up."

"How did she end up in a shower curtain?"

"The shower curtain? That was my idea." He grinned at his own cleverness.

"What about the cinder blocks?"

"That was Cassidy. We saw them in the back yard, along the fence. He figured two would do it, so I picked them up and put 'em in the trunk, next to the blanket. Loco and me, we had her all wrapped up and taped up in the shower curtain already, before Mister Cassidy got there. He just wanted her in the blanket. Didn't want her to show, I guess."

"Thanks," Redding said. "Either of you want anything to drink? Soda? Coffee? We're going to talk about the Cassidy murder next." Neither was thirsty, so Redding launched into the next inquiry.

"You didn't come down here with Ippolito to go to some pizza party," he began, "so why did you come here last week?"
"Mister Ippolito said we might have to get some information from Mister Cassidy," Loverne said. "He didn't say what about, just

we might have to get rough. I didn't buy it. I
mean – that little creep?"

"So, what did happen?"

"Well, Ippolito told Loco to wait out back
until he heard Cassidy in the house, 'cuz he
thought he might run. Then Loco was supposed
to block the front door. And he did run out, but
Loco was right there, and he walked him back
in and sat him down."

"Did Cassidy admit to anything? Like,
skimming money from either Pullman or your
boss?"

"Yeah, sorta. But we all know he did it."

"How much money?"

"It was a lot. A couple hundred thousand? I
don't know, exactly. But it was a lot of money."

"So what happened next?"

"Well…"

"What happened next, Loverne? No deal if
you don't tell me everything."

Ferguson leaned into the suspect and said
softly, "You might as well tell him everything.
The only way this could get worse for you is if
you don't."

"Well… well, Mister Pullman and Mister
Ippolito kinda looked at each other. I was
standing behind Mister Cassidy. He was on
the couch. Mister Ippolito just nodded at me."

228

"Was that some kind of signal?"

"Yeah. It was like his code. I grabbed Mister Cassidy's head, and gave it a quick turn and a pull. Snapped it. His neck."

"You have used this 'code' before?"

"It was understood."

"Ippolito didn't say anything?"

"Didn't have to. I knew what he wanted."

"Sorry. I need to be clear. Ippolito didn't say anything at all?"

"No. Like I say, he didn't have to."

"Okay. So then, what happened?"

"So then Loco an' me, we put Mister Cassidy in the trunk."

"Was he dead at this time?"

"Yeah, dead. And we came back into the house. Mister Ippolito told us he never wanted to see us again, that we should never come back to Chicago. To go to Cleveland, where he would tell us what to do when we got there. He told me -- me, not Loco -- that I could have the car. He'd mail me the title in Cleveland. And he said to leave the plates – Illinois has two plates, front and back – before we went. So Loco took the plates off and brought them in, and I took the rest of Mister Ippolito's stuff out of the car and the glove compartment, and brought all that stuff in, and he told us to get moving. So we did."

"You drove?"

"Yeah. Loco's got too many points. So he drove the BMW."

"Cassidy's car? Did you take Cassidy's wallet, anything from his body?"

"Yeah, his BMW. No. Nothing. We were in a hurry, and Mister Ippolito didn't ask for anything. We didn't really think about it. I didn't even think about it until now."

"Do you think Ippolito tipped them off?"

"Well, yeah, of course. And here I am, taking the rap for him, while he's walking around free. And Pullman's already gone home, and he started the whole thing."

"Loco's on the hook, too, if that makes you feel better."

"Yeah, right. Loco isn't white, either, in case you didn't notice."

Redding addressed Ferguson. "You have another client with another appointment." He looked at Loverne. "Thank you, Mister Washington. And we'll need you to tell the truth again in open court, so Ippolito and Pullman don't get away with something. And if you think of any other details, please let me know."

Loverne started out the door with the guard, looked back, and said, "It's all four of us go down, or nobody. Not half and half. If I'm guilty an' Loco's guilty, they're guilty."

Chapter Seventeen: Turning Loco

Stumpf took the lead with Loco. With Redding's notes spread before him, questioning went similarly, except for some details of Jean Leitner's murder.

"We caught her downstairs, taped up her mouth. When she goes like 'yes, I'll talk,' we pull the tape off her mouth, but she doesn't say anything. Just, she don't know about no stash. She got away at the top of the stairs, but we caught her on the bed and…"

"You pushed her into the bathtub?" Stumpf asked.

Loco was surprised that Stumpf knew. "Yeah. I held her down, and Loverne hit her a couple times, but she kept saying she didn't know about no stash. Says she made it up."

"What did you do then?"

"Loverne, he told me to hold her down. I was already holding her down, but he got crazy, and he started pulling her teeth out. Even when she tried to talk, he kept doin' it, and she passed out. He told me 'bring her back,' but I didn't know what to do. That's when he chopped off her hand. She opened her eyes, but she didn't say nothing. Then she passed out again. Loverne, man, he was like an animal. He pulled out all her teeth, but she didn't wake up. He screamed at her, but nothing. Then he grabbed her other hand and – shit! – he cut that one off, too."

Stumpf remained silent. Loco was on a roll, and kept going.

"Loverne, man, he tol' me to clean her up. She wasn't bleeding too much, then. She's already in the tub, so I just turned on the water and washed myself off. Her, too. I was crying. We didn't find the stash, and now she's dead. Mister Ippolito would be mad. So, anyway, we pulled the shower curtain down and wrapped her up in it, duc' taped her real good. And Loverne called Mister Cassidy, and he came over."

"How did she end up in the blanket?"

"Mister Cassidy, he brought up the blanket. I guess from his car. We wrapped her up in that, too. More duc' tape. Then we put her in the trunk of the car. The keys were on a table downstairs. We followed Mister Cassidy to Burger King." And Loco's story matched Loverne's from there.

"Anything else? Did you see Mister Leitner?"

"Oh, yeah. He was sleeping in the other bedroom. I went in there to get a shoe, so Loverne could chop and not chip his blade. He used it like, what do you call those?"

234

"A cutting board?"

"Yeah, like you make salad on. He used his shoe."

"Where were the hands and teeth?"

"Loverne tol' me to get all that stuff into his bag, to wash 'em good first. I put everything in there – the shoe, his chopper, the shoe, Missus Leitner's…"

"Her hands?"

"Yeah, and her teeth. The duc' tape from around her head, with the hair on it. Everything. Then I cleaned up the tub. That's when Mister Cassidy got there. So then we did all that, that I told you about."

"What did you do with her car?"

"Loverne drove it to Chicago. I drove our car."

Stumpf acted puzzled. "I thought you didn't drive."

"I have too many points, so I didn't want to get caught driving a stolen car, besides."

"What did you do with it in Chicago?"

"Loverne sold it to a guy he knows. Got a thousand."

"Each?"

"No. Five hundred each."

Then Stumpf lied a little. "He told me he got three grand for it."

Loco didn't respond immediately. Then he said, "Well, I guess I don' remember so good."

Stumpf switched his questioning to pizza night at Pullman's, where Loco's story substantially matched Loverne's.

Then the detective said, "If you remember anything else, you'll be sure to tell me, right?"

Cathy Ferguson answered, "Yes, Detective, he certainly will." Then she pushed back her chair and said to Loco, "Okay, you've done your part. Let's go."

Stumpf reminded Loco, "Remember, if you change your story in court or if your memory goes bad, the deal is off, and you'll get the death penalty."

Loco grunted and disappeared down the hall with the guard and his lawyer.

Chapter Eighteen: Irritating Phillips

Ippolito's lawyer from Chicago arrived. He was fifty-something, tall, with a huge mane of salt-and-pepper atop an athletic frame. A principal in a boutique criminal law firm, Phillips had been around the block in his handmade suits and polished Guccis. An attractive thirty-something blonde assistant, dressed in a severe but snug dark blue suit, carried his briefcase.

"I am Thomas Phillips," he announced at the front desk. "I am here to secure the immediate release of my client, Adriano Ippolito."

"Please have a seat, Mister Phillips." Connie indicated a row or chairs along the wall, but Phillips didn't move as she called Detective Redding. "Jerry, Mister Ippolito's lawyer is here."

Redding and Plessy arrived together and introduced themselves. "How long have you been in town, Mister Thomas?" Redding chided, dead serious.

"It's Thomas Phillips. I've just arrived. Shall we get down to business?"

"Well, Thomas," Redding continued, playing the small-town hayseed, "I'm afraid you'll need to come back in the morning. It's ten after five, see, and well, it's past quitting time, and I can't ask all these nice people here to work extra. Besides, it's not in the budget, you know."

Redding looked at Plessy and asked, puppy-eyed, "Is there any way we can work a little extra today?"

Plessy felt like choking, but played his part. "It's already too late to ask. And the judge went home an hour ago." Then he turned to Phillips. "I'm sorry to inconvenience you, Mister Thomas, but…"

"It's Phillips."

"Oh, right. Sorry. Sorry, Mister Phillips, but we have some very strict rules about overtime here, and I'm not authorized to just break them. But we'll be open again at eight sharp, and we'll see you then."

Redding added, "As a courtesy, though, I'll tell Mister Ippolito you arrived okay, just a couple minutes too late. See you in the morning."

Phillips whirled around and stormed out, his assistant barely keeping up with him, her tight skirt and heels restricting her to numerous baby steps as detective and ADA paid attention.

When they cleared the second door, Plessy and Redding exchanged smiles and a fist bump, but not a word.

Connie let go a giggle. "Good night, gentlemen," she said, still smiling as she headed for the time clock at the back door.

The detective and the ADA worked until nine-thirty, preparing a solid argument against the release on bond of Adriano Ippolito.

* * *

But in the morning's arraignment, Ippolito was released to the custody of Phillips, on two hundred thousand dollars' bond, with a hearing date a month hence.

"Follow them?" Stumpf asked, already heading for the garage.

"Absolutely," said Redding, as he kicked the nearest wastebasket. "And I'm going to have to pick up Pullman. I don't want them getting together on this."

As he went to his office, he said to Connie, "Can you get me everything on Pullman's loan to my brother?"

He called Plessy, who said he could get an arrest warrant, and before lunch, Pullman was back, this time without the option of leaving at will. He was furious as Redding entered the interrogation room. "What the hell, Detective?" he asked. "I thought we were done here." 239

"No, not until the guilty are all behind bars," Redding explained. "And you beat up my brother."

"I want my lawyer," said a defiant Pullman.

"And who is that, since your lawyer, near as I can tell, is the guy we found in the trunk of your friend's 'stolen' car?"

"Just call Erickson and Eckersoll," he said. "They'll send somebody. In the meantime, I'm not saying anything."

"As you wish," Redding said, and left the room, Pullman still secured to the steel table.

* * *

Redding went back to his office and watched the interrogation room's camera on his monitor. He dialed his brother.

"Look, Charlie," he was saying after a curt hello, "I am really sorry that happened, and I know I'm guilty as sin, setting you up. I'm going to get that son of a bitch, not just for all the other stuff he did, but especially for what he did to you. It's personal, understand? But I need your help… Yeah, I know I don't deserve it, but you want to see him fry, don't you? … Yeah, maybe I'll fry too, but later. First we get Pullman, okay? Can you come in and make a statement?"

Twenty minutes later, Connie called Redding and told him his brother was in with Plessy.

"Hi, Charlie, you're looking good," Redding said to the back of his half-brother's head, as he walked into Plessy's office without knocking.

Charlie Newman turned around to look at him. "Shut up, Jerry," he said. "I'm here on police business." Then he turned again to Plessy, and the older brother left silently, the latch barely making a sound as the door gently closed.

* * *

Redding called Stumpf. "Fred, can we get anything useful out of Ronnie McGowan, the kid that worked for Cassidy?"

"I don't know, Jerry. I haven't paid any attention to him. Seems like all he did was carry money and messages."

"With Cassidy dead, maybe he'll remember something useful. See if he knows anything that can help us... Thanks."

Then Redding laid out what Pullman and Ippolito had against the other: *Pullman didn't get the stash. There wasn't any stash. But he got connected to three murders, because Ippolito's guys didn't know when to back down. And that wasn't their fault. It was Ippolito's.*

Ippolito got involved in two murders and had heavy expenses that he wasn't likely to get paid for. And he had lost two men, all thanks to Pullman's bad information and stupid ideas.

And both were in danger of being convicted for capital murder, thanks to the other man. Neither would want to go down alone, but each would try to clear himself. And that would benefit the other. What will it take to get one to attack the other? Who has the most – or the least -- to lose? How can I provoke a fight?

Ippolito's going down, regardless. He has nothing to lose. It's all Pullman's fault. Blame Pullman.

Chapter Nineteen:
Pullman leaves the station

The next morning, Stumpf arrived late and angry. He threw his jacket on his desk and kept walking to Redding, in the next office. "Jerry, bad news."

"We're cops, Fred. Bad news is our bread and butter. What's your news?"

"Pullman's not at home. His wife's not seen him since yesterday afternoon. He told her he was going to a client meeting, maybe be late. Don't wait up. She didn't."

"She called us?"

"No. I dropped by to see our tail, and he was asleep. Said he didn't know when he dozed off."

"Where…"

"Outside Saint Salmon's, the seafood restaurant."

"So our guy slept through the night?"

"Apparently. Said he remembers being awake, for sure, about nine thirty last night. I woke him up at eight, today. Had the radio off."

"Well, HR has a problem and he's got a problem, but we've got a huge problem. Who was he meeting with?"

"Our Inspector Clouseau doesn't have a clue. Never looked inside, didn't recognize any guests."

"Cameras?"

"Not working for the last week."

"Anybody there remember anything?"

"They're not open until four. Maybe someone will remember. I only talked with the manager on the phone."

"Did he pay cash or card?"

"No bank records match Pullman at Salmon's last night. Either he paid cash, or his guest picked up the check. Maybe they didn't run the card batch last night, or maybe the bank hasn't run last night's posts. We'll know more, later today. But I doubt it."

Redding leaned back. "I should have known that ahead of time, shouldn't I? So, he has twelve, fifteen hours on us, plenty of cash, and good reason to disappear. He didn't tell his wife, er… what's her name? Vanessa – anything?"

Fred said, "If you were disappearing, would you?"

* * *

"Ronnie," Redding said into his cell phone. "Ronnie McGowan? Detective Jerry Redding… No, you're not in trouble. I've got a couple questions maybe you can help me with, about your old boss, Barry Cassidy. You working these days?... Okay, can you come in?... Yeah, now is good. Thanks."

Ronnie was prompt and unshaven, dressed in t-shirt and jeans, smelling like yesterday's sweat. "I got here as fast as I could, Detective."

"Good. Thanks. Coffee?" Redding yelled out the door to whoever might be there, "Bring us two coffees, please, anybody. Black. Right away. Thanks."

He focused on Ronnie. "What are you, twenty-three? Twenty-four?"

"Twenty-six, actually. I laid out of school a while. Look young, I guess."

"Look, Ronnie, we are still working on your boss's murder, and the ones he might have been in on."

"Yeah, I know. What do you want from me?"

"I want you to think of anybody you remember that you ever saw with Pullman. At his house, at Barry Cassidy's office…"

"He never came to the office."

"Okay, with him at a restaurant, anybody who might know him."

"Man, he was always at home, mostly. I do remember him and Barry and Barry's girlfriend together at some restaurant, fancy place. Barry called me in to tell me he was going to be using her sometimes, and I shouldn't get upset. There was plenty of work to go around."

"Who was that? What was she like?"

"Nice girl. Blonde, talked a lot. I don't think Mister Pullman would have approved, except..."

"Yeah, except what?"

"She was real pooty. Big boobs, tiny waist. Nice legs, short skirt. Cute, really cute. Short, tiny."

How old?"

"About my age. Middle twenties."

"Do you remember her name?"

"Kind of an old fashioned name. Carly. Cathy. Something with a K or a C..."

"Carlene?"

"Coulda been. I don't remember her name, but I'd remember her if I saw her again."

Redding pushed a photo across the desk, something he had pulled from CrazyHotChicks.com. "This her?"

"Yeah, that's her. Nice picture."

"Yeah, her name's Carlene. I'd like it if you could make yourself an introduction to her, see if she knows more about the business Pullman and your old boss had. We'll pay."

"My pleasure. Go after her, on your expense account?"

"Hold your horses, cowboy. Just a couple dates. Then you're on your own, so don't spoil her too much, or you'll be stuck with promises your wallet won't be able to keep. But yes. Here's why. Pullman's kinda disappeared, and we think he's still local. He's always at home, except when he was with Barry, and well, he's not with Barry any more. So she's the next best thing we've got to a lead."

Ronnie just kept looking at the picture.

"So, you want to do it?"

"Uh, sure. But I…"

"I know, you wouldn't feel right about getting into this situation alone, so I've got a partner for you, sorta keep you focused."

"I can do it alone."

"Ronnie, do you have a Private Investigator's license?"

"Well, no, but…"

"But nothing. You do this right, you're on your way to getting on with a good PI outfit, maybe becoming one yourself. Are you in?"

"Well, okay. What's the pay, and all that?"

"We'll work that out with your partner. Can you be here at three this afternoon? Cleaned up?"

"Sure, Detective. Will do."

"See you at three."

* * *

Redding took a deep breath and dialed. "Charlie? Yeah… no, I'm not calling to get you killed. I need…" *Son of a bitch.* Redding dialed again. "Charlie, what I meant to say is, I have a way for you to get revenge… No, not on me. On Pullman… He's skipped. You're still licensed, right? You want him?... Okay, here's what I've got."

Redding filled him in, and finished with, "So, come meet your new partner here. Three o'clock… Thanks. Really, thanks."

* * *

Charlie looked at the skinny kid and introduced himself. "I'm also Detective Redding's half-brother, and Chip Pullman gave me this shiner and the broken cheekbone to go with it. He plays rough, and the police can't protect you," he said, glancing at Redding. "Understand?"

"Yes, sir. I'm not afraid of Mister Pullman."

"Well, I'm… let's say I respect him. He's dangerous, and his friends are dangerous. But if we don't get him right away, he might disappear for good."

"So, what can I do to help?"

"First, we're going to canvas the places he might have gone. You know some of them, right?"

"Not really. I know a couple of places Mister Cassidy went…"

"Well, you'll have a partner. We're all going to find a few of his likeliest hideouts, and you two will stake out some, while I follow up on others."

"Why do I need a partner, and you don't?"

"Because I'm a PI and you're not. It'll take both your heads to do the same amount of work." Then Charlie Newman asked his young partner, "Hungry?"

"Always."

"Okay." He turned to Redding. "We're leaving. Got work to do."

Chapter Twenty: A team of misfits

"Get in." They piled into Newman's beat-up Fiesta, and he headed for the Burger King. "Might as well go where everything started." Over two Double Whopper Meals, Newman took the measure of McGowan. "What do you plan on getting out of this, Ronnie?"

"Just help catch the bad guy, I guess."

"Any thoughts of taking over your old boss's business?"

"What business – lawyering or collections? I'm not a lawyer…"

"Collections. You've already got a start."

"I didn't get near the clients. I just ran the money and messages around town."

"Exactly. You know the layout. You know who's looking for money, who can't get it, who can. You know how it's done, even if you never did it yourself." Newman chomped down on another mouthful of bun, salad, beef, and condiments. "That makes you valuable to somebody, and it gives you a good chance to start your own business. Once we catch Pullman, he won't be a problem, and Cassidy? No problem there, either. I mean, who else even knows what Cassidy was doing, really?"

"Nobody, I guess. Except maybe his girlfriend. She may look like a dingy cheerleader, but she's smart."

"You think she knew what Cassidy was into?"

"To some degree, yes. I walked in on them a couple times – in the office, I mean – and I think he was using her somehow in the business." He gulped his diet cola. "Why are you asking me all this?"

"Because," Newman said, "I want to know who I'm working with, if it's just a one-shot thing or part of a plan. I want to know that I can count on you, trust you. This guy, Pullman," he rubbed his cheekbone, "Pullman is serious as shit. People die around him. And he already doesn't like me. Figures I owe him fourteen, plus interest. Plus I'm the detective's brother, and I was setting him up."

"Yeah, you're serious, all right. Me? Honestly? Right now, I just want a job. Who's this partner you were talking about?"

"Cassidy's old girlfriend, Carlene Gunther."

"You mean the…?"

"Yeah, her." He looked straight into Ronnie's eyes. "Look, Ronnie. You do this one right, and you'll not only get paid, you'd be on the road to getting laid. 'Course that's up to you."

Ronnie dropped a french fry into the puddle of ketchup on the spread-out paper wrapper. "What do you want me to do?"

* * *

"Hello, Carlene Gunther? …Yes, right. You don't know me. I'm Charlie Newman. I'm the brother of Jerry Redding, the detective who's working on Barry Cassidy's murder. I'm a private investigator, and I've been hired to find Chip Pullman."

"Chip Pullman? That bastard? Why are you calling me?"

"Because you might know something about his habits or his business, someone he knows, where he might be."

"He's probably in Barbados, or Mexico, or someplace. Not here."

"Why do you think he's gone?"

"Why do you think he's still around?" Newman said, "I think he's still here. He has plenty of locals who owe him favors. He didn't have time to clean out his bank accounts. And frankly, he just doesn't have that much business out of the country. He's a regional loan shark, not a big international fish. So, why do you think he's gone?"

"I don't know. It just seems that with everybody here looking for him, he'd want to get as far away as possible."

253

"But no solid reasons?"

"No."

"Listen, Carlene. I'd like to sit down with you somewhere, have you meet the rest of the team. See if there's anything we all can do, to get this guy. Can you meet me at The Grill, down in the Lucaya Landing shops, in half an hour?"

"An hour, I can."

"Good. See you there."

Then he called Ronnie.

* * *

Charlie picked a table along the back wall, opposite corner from the kitchen, where the background noise wasn't too loud. Ronnie showed up, still dressed for success from the three o'clock, but now reeking of Vanilla Smoke cologne.

"Gawd, Ronnie. What's that you're wearing? Smells like a burned milk shake."

"It's supposed to. It's cool. Glad we're in a mall. I stopped at Nordstrom's and got a shot of the sample stuff."

"Just hope it doesn't make her sneeze… oh -- she's here."

Both men stood up, and Carlene came over and introduced herself. She was wearing a knee-length but tight black vinyl skirt that was supposed to look like leather and a light-blue summer-knit long-sleeve turtleneck with a zipper all the way down the front, with a big ring pull, which was positioned precisely at mid-breast height, and a little gold chain belt, not attached to anything but hanging loosely on her hips. Charlie strained hard to maintain eye contact. Ronnie failed, pretending to look at the table or maybe his shoes, but he was fixated on that zipper ring. He snapped out of the trance as Charlie pulled out her chair and made a theatrical gesture for her to join them.

"So, how do we get this guy?" she said, as everyone sat down and the waiter brought the drink menu.

Charlie waved him away. "No drinks," he said. Then, to Carlene, "We think he's still around. If not actually in town, then close. His business was pretty much all local. He didn't seem to want to tangle with bigger fish, or get into their ponds."

Carlene nodded. "I've been thinking about it all the way over here. Barry didn't talk much about names, but he liked me to ride along with him, sort of show me off to people. Arm-candy stuff. He's ten years older than me. He was thinking I didn't know what he was doing."

"What was he doing?"

"He used me to keep the marks off balance, while he pulled deals on them."

Ronnie said, "I bet it worked."

She shot him a glance. "Barry didn't have any female clients. Not that I ever saw, anyway."

Charlie said, "So, you don't know who these people are? You don't remember their names?"

"They didn't use names. Just 'friend,' 'brother,' sometimes 'asshole.' No names. But I've lived in this town all my life. I know where they live. I remember faces. I can show you."

Ronnie said, "Did Barry ever get rough with them?"

"I never saw him do anything," Carlene said. "Never even raised his voice. He just made it sound like he had 'people' behind him, 'people' that the clients wouldn't want to meet. That worked, I guess. I mean, we were already in their homes."

Dinner was marvelous, but Charlie surmised that Carlene didn't really love Barry. She liked the adventure of his job, his money, the attention of an older man. She justified the relationship by telling herself this was her job, that she was getting paid in cash for some kind of internship with benefits. "But mostly his benefits," she said. "But don't get me wrong.

He was real nice to me. Liked me more than I liked him, but I guess that's why I was getting paid, to make up for the difference."

No one had dessert. Charlie said, "When do you want to get started?"

"Am I getting paid?"Ronnie looked at Charlie, pleading for him to be generous.

Charlie said, "Yeah. The pay is ten thousand, half the bond money. So it's good, if we catch him fast. Not so good, if it takes too long. And nothing, if somebody else gets him first. We split it fifty, twenty-five, twenty-five."

"Why?" Ronnie wanted to know.

"Because I got the job, and I'm the one with the PI license. And I'm paying for dinner. Consider this an internship. If we catch Pullman in a week, that's twenty-five hundred for a week's work. That's, uhhh… a hundred and thirty thousand dollars a year. Not bad for an intern."

Ronnie said, "What if it takes two weeks?"

Carlene looked at Charlie. Then she grabbed Ronnie's arm and led him out of the restaurant, like a mother with a recalcitrant child, albeit a child a foot taller than she was. "If it takes two weeks, he'll be gone. Let's go."

* * *

"I can't be totally sure in the dark," Carlene said, after the trio had driven to a few locations she remembered, that Charlie and Ronnie documented. "Everything looks different. Can we do this in the morning? Early?"

"Like six-thirty," Charlie said. "We'll meet at the strip mall, at the end, where Barry's office was. You," he looked in the back seat at Ronnie, but Carlene knew he meant her, too, "you grab food and coffee before you get there. We're not going on any breakfast run. We need every minute."

Chapter Twenty-One: Who's crazy?

Plessy and Ferguson were playing chess, playing with Loco and Loverne's futures as if they were a couple pawns.

"Look, Cathy. Your clients killed at least two people. They're each blaming the other, but all that does is put them both at the crime scene and show their intent. They're going to be convicted. In this state, that can be the death penalty."

"I know the law, Jacob, and I know what they did, but I'm not as sure as you are that the juries will see it that way. Loco, he's crazy, crazy from youth. You can bring in your shrinks. I can bring mine, and family, teachers, friends. If I can't get him off altogether, I can certainly get him committed. And if he's crazy, your case against Loverne is a lot weaker. So, do you want to try Loverne first, or Loco?"

"No. Ippolito first. The defense will try to disqualify Loco and Loverne as witnesses. Loco for being crazy, Loverne as a disgruntled – to say the least -- employee, but both your guys hate him. You know Loco won't want to lose his chance to take Ippolito down. He's going to act plenty sane for Ippolito's trial. And that's how he's going to be found: sane. And you'd best not be interfering with witnesses in my trial."

"So, what are you offering?"

"Loverne and Loco get a chance to see Ippolito go down, and a chance to show that they're cooperating."

"…and that gets them, what, exactly?"

"That gets them sympathy in their trials. 'Poor dumb minorities, exploited by the white, Italian – Mafia, maybe? -- boss.' They might get life, or even just a conviction on lesser charges. Provided Ippolito is found guilty. And your man Loco can't be crazy."

"What, exactly, are you offering?"

"Nothing, 'exactly.' Not until after Ippolito and Pullman face justice."

"So why are we talking?" Ferguson said.

"Because I want you to know that Ippolito and Pullman mean a lot more to me than Loverne and Loco. Just sayin'."

"And what the hell does that mean, Jacob?" But Plessy was leaving, and didn't reply.

* * *

"Tree," Redding said, "we've got to get these cases in order for the prosecution. Start with Pullman. What've we got? Just the facts."

"Jerry, I see a loan shark who figures out that he's being cheated by his own collector, his own lawyer, a guy he's helped all of his adult life, a guy he sees as his beneficiary, a guy he's been generous with, a guy he trusted. Now he's betrayed. Lied to, stolen from. Had his business undermined. Cost him money, made him visible to us. Pullman had sadness, anger, distrust, hate for Cassidy. Pullman is a bully, not a murderer. He doesn't know how to handle that. That's why he gets Ippolito into the game."

"Let's stick with Pullman. Opportunity?"

"Pizza party, with four against one."

"Motivation, you've already covered. And the means?"

"You already said it. Four against one." Redding said, "Okay, so what are we missing, and what else we got?"

"We're missing a smoking gun. The cat hairs make the case for you and me, connecting Jean Leitner to Barry Cassidy to Pullman's cat, but the cat hairs are circumstantial."

"That's the Leitner murder, not Cassidy, anyway."

"Our biggest case rests on Ippolito, Loco, and Loverne's stories. But let's get back to the rest of it.

Redding said, "And they all hate Pullman for one reason or another. But they're all connected in the murder, too. What if they all refuse to testify?"

Stumpf asked, "Hey, did Pullman go to the Bahamas lately?"

"What? Umm, no, we didn't see him out of the country for at least four years. Why?"

"But Cassidy did, six weeks ago, for a weekend thing with Carlene."

"And?"

"And the Bahamas is the only place you can buy Sands beer. They don't export. Sands beer bottles were in Pullman's trash. And one bottle in the fridge. With recent product dates."

"So Cassidy brought the beer to his own funeral?"

"Right. That's one more thing that puts Cassidy at Pullman's on the night he got killed, in case any of the witnesses get cold feet."

"Okay, that's good. Plus, we have their tapes, where they incriminated Pullman."

"…and incriminated themselves," Stumpf said.

"The Fifth doesn't cover that, and maybe a lawyer could confuse the jury about it, and if the judge doesn't explain it – and why should he? – the jury could get confused."

"Okay, Jerry. We have the pizza that matches the pizza in Cassidy's gullet. Same pizza Pullman gave you. Those beer bottles. Cassidy in the trunk of Ippolito's car."

"Loverne and Loco killed Cassidy, put his body in the trunk, and stole the car, remember?"

"Makes no sense. They didn't have anything against Cassidy. That whole story makes no sense, anyway."

"Cassidy could have dropped the dime on them for Jean Leitner's murder. I mean, they did it and all."

"Sure, Jerry, it's circumstantial evidence, but it's irrefutable. The story that Pullman's in the bathroom when Cassidy, Loverne, and Loco vanish in Ippolito's car – they stole their boss's car? – is impossible to believe."

"And Ippolito was in the bathroom at the same time, remember?"

"Yeah, crowded in there, another chunk of BS. All the recorded testimony points in the same direction. And the pizza matches. And Cassidy hasn't been dead an hour when they're caught on the highway. Oh, and Ippolito knew exactly where to look for his car, and their stories both say he told them to go there."

"It's Plessy's job now," Redding said, as he closed the file on Pullman. "And it's our job to find him."

Chapter Twenty-Two:
Cruisin' and bruisin'

Carlene wore her blonde hair under a baseball cap. T-shirt and yoga pants and a gigantic cloth purse completed her ensemble. Ronnie and Charlie were already in the car. Charlie popped her door open from inside. "Got your eyes on?" Charlie asked.

"Let's roll," Carlene said.

Ronnie, from the back seat, with the camera, said, "Where we goin'?"

"Canterbury Acres first. I figured I'd start with the ones I remember for sure. Maybe that'll jog my memory for some that I just kinda remember."

Charlie turned through the brick gateway onto Canterbury Lane, modern McMansions on both sides of the street, with barely enough space between them to put up two fences for the show dogs everyone seemed to have in their back yards.

"Turn right," she said. The winding street gave those on the inside of the curve wide front lawns, and the widest was in front of the first house she tagged. A three-story tract house with a fake Tudor façade, painted white stucco, three-car garage. There," she said.

"That's one of them."

"You sure?" Ronnie said, as he wrote down the address and snapped a photo.

"Positive. Keep going, same street, to the end. It ends at a T. Turn left, then slow down." She found another 'for sure' there, a red brick ranch that had more lot than house. It looked out of place.

It went on all morning, different neighborhoods. Three more 'for sures,' four 'maybes.'

* * *

At one o'clock or a little after, Charlie drove to a Cracker Barrel, down by the Interstate. "Hard work all morning," he said. "You've earned some true luxury."

Ronnie, who had said he never went anywhere with Cassidy, also remembered three of the houses, two of the 'for sures' Carlene spotted, and one of her 'maybes,' one he was positive about. Charlie didn't have time to give them a full course in surveillance, so he boiled it down to a few sentences.

"We have two prime targets – the ones you both tagged -- and five total, and people enough to watch three. What I want to do," Charlie said, "is put each of you on one of the two, and I'll have to float the other three. Carlene, you do the

Canterbury Lane house. Ronnie, Overlook Drive. As close to twenty-four hours as you can. Don't be obvious. Don't park too close, or in the same place, or facing the same direction – you can use the rear-view mirror, too. Park and walk sometimes. Wear different things – one day, you're a bicyclist, the next day, a jogger or a student with a backpack. Switch cars with each other."

"Find out whatever else you can about the household – see if they're buying things that don't fit. He's gonna need clothes, but he won't be getting tailored stuff. Watch for Walmart and Target bags coming into the house. Especially when the garage door opens, look inside for his Mercedes. It's a red, two-seat, sports car convertible, tan top. And look for anything unusual or that doesn't make sense. Anything – remember, you aren't likely to see Pullman himself. Call me immediately if you think you have anything."

"Oh, and bring some bread and cheese and water. You don't want to be taking snack breaks every two hours. No reading material. No DVD players. Stay off your phones unless you're calling me, and only you've got something. Don't get made. Questions?... Then let's go."

* * *

Two hours later, Charlie's phone rang. "It's Ronnie. Hey, I'm on Overlook drive, and I was about four doors down from the house, and this guy across the street where I'm parked, he comes out of his garage in a red Mercedes convertible, tan roof."

"Did you see the guy?"

"No, but I got the plate. GN two thousand one."

"Where is he now?"

"Want me to follow him?"

"Good one, Ronnie. That's his car. Go, go, go. And stay on the phone. Where are you, exactly? Can you see him?"

"North on Monroe, passing Main. Not going very fast. Pulling over in front of the barber shop, a block north of Main. He's going in."

"Okay. Go right on by, turn the corner, then make a U turn and face back to Monroe, so you can just see him. Hang up now. I'm calling the cops."

Charlie called Jerry, who told him to head to the location and watch, but not get close, as the arrest team was scrambled.

Ronnie continued to watch the Mercedes, eyes to the left, not missing anything until a loud tapping on the passenger-side window snapped his head around. Ronnie was looking at a gun. "Open the door," said a gruff voice, as the gun waved at him.

Pullman climbed in. "Drive," he said. Ronnie turned left on Monroe, going past the parked Mercedes as a police car headed in his direction. Without making it obvious, Ronnie flashed his brights at the squad car, but Ronnie sighed as it went right by and pulled over behind the Mercedes. Pullman saw the police, too. Said, "Chip doesn't live there anymore. Keep driving. Straight to the bypass, then get on, westbound."

Five minutes later, as Ronnie was turning left to get on the Interstate ramp, some stupid blonde in an old Pontiac ran the red light and T-boned his car. Pullman's hip was broken and his head hit the door's window, then the dashboard. He dropped the gun, and Ronnie got out of his seat belt, picked up the Colt auto and gave Pullman's head a whack with it. Then another one for insurance.

Police cars converged from all directions, and an ambulance crew strapped Pullman securely to a gurney and took him, with two officers, to Mercy Hospital.

Ronnie walked over to the blonde with the wrecked Pontiac and gave her a huge hug. "That was good thinking. Thanks." He said, "How did you…"

"You dope," she said. Carlene grabbed his butt with her right hand, the back of his head with her left, and pulled her to him, kissing him hard.

He staggered, but for just a moment, and recovered, placing one hand behind her, at the base of her neck; his other went around her small waist. They held each other in this tight hug until oxygen deprivation weakened them, and his hands went to her hips, hers behind his neck. They looked at each other, arms' length, surprised. "You called me. I heard the whole thing and realized I was right there, so I just... ran into you." She gave a silly smile, like running into him was the most natural thing in the world. "Call me, okay? I'll be needing a ride for a while."

Ronnie said, "Sure. Yeah, of course. That's right. I had just called you when he showed up. Put the phone in my shirt pocket when he knocked on the window. Thanks, by the way." Then, without reflecting on his own wreck, he stepped back and said, "I'll take you anywhere you want to go."

* * *

Back at the station, the five – Charlie, Ronnie, Carlene, and the two detectives – ordered pizza and went to the break room for a long debrief.

270

Redding started. "Well, Pullman's not going to run any time soon. It's official: his right hip is broken. He hit his head on something, too. Got a nasty couple cuts there. Hey, Ronnie, you got insurance for a passenger?"

He said, "I don't care, as long as Carlene does."

Carlene said, "You're not going to give me a ticket or anything, are you?" and they all laughed.

Fred Stumpf said, "Sure we are. You ran a red light and failed to yield. Then you left the scene of an accident with injuries. You're looking at five to ten at State." Her face fell. He laughed. Everybody laughed. "Seriously, that was quick thinking, and we're grateful. You two," looking at Carlene, then Ronnie, "are getting the reward. Fifty thousand dollars."

Charlie shot a look at Jerry. "You still get your ten," Jerry said. "And you still get to keep your five of it. The kids here need the dough to get some new wheels. Besides, you promised, right?"

"Right. Yeah, thanks, bro."

The pizza arrived. Stumpf paid, went out as they opened it up, then came back with sodas. He raised his Diet Coke in a toast. "Let's hope nobody gags on this pizza." Soda cans clicked and the pizza was quickly dismembered and devoured, as the serious business of getting all the cards on the table commenced.

After the others left, Stumpf made an offhand remark. "She's kinda sweet on Ronnie."

"Well," said Redding, "he's a nice kid. Nerdy. Maybe she likes that."

"Nerdy …and broke. Cassidy was rich, comparatively. She's like, going from caviar to… cheese from a spray can."

"They sell a lot more spray cheese than caviar, Tree."

It was nearly midnight when Redding and Stumpf finished. Redding left a message for Plessy about call him first thing in the morning.

Chapter Twenty-three: Bathroom bingo

Pullman, despite the IV drip in obvious pain on the hospital bed, wanted to explain to Stumpf that his head injuries were because Ronnie McGowan whacked him on the head with his own gun, but he couldn't think of a way to do that without making his case worse. He just lay there, appreciating the Demerol and evading the questions as best he could, answering even as his attorney said he was on his way.

Pullman didn't help himself. "I didn't know that kid worked for you," he said. "Thought he might be wanting to rob me, stalking me like he was."

"Did you call in the stalker?" Stumpf asked. "Well, no. I knew you were looking for me." He pointed to his IV bag. "This stuff isn't that good."

"So, what did you want, when you got into the car with him?"

"I just wanted to find out who he was at first. Then I think I just wanted him to get me out of town."

"Where were you going?"

"I didn't really have a plan. But I figured if he could find me, so could you. And I thought maybe you thought by then I was already long gone, so you wouldn't have roadblocks, be looking for me here."

"We would have found you, anyway."

"I can't believe you used that stupid McGowan kid."

"He could recognize you. You may think he's not too bright, but he caught you. As for 'using' him, why wouldn't we? Besides, he didn't have a job any more, remember? He used to work for Cassidy, but Cassidy's dead. Had some kind of problem at your house."

"I didn't have anything to do with that."

"Do you have an alibi?"

"Yeah. I was in the bathroom when he left. I told you that."

"Yeah, I mean, do you have anybody who could back that up?"

"My friend, the Chicago lawyer, Adriano Ippolito."

"Funny."

"What's funny?"

"He was in the bathroom, same time as you. Was he in the same bathroom? How many bathrooms do you have, between the front room and the kitchen?"

"He must have been in the other bathroom. I was alone."

"Was he still in the front room when you left for the bathroom?"

"Yes. I remember saying to him I'd be right back and if he wanted another beer."

"Did he answer?"

"He didn't want a beer. Then I went."

"Did you urinate or defecate?"

"What?"

"Did you poop or pee?"

"Peed. Why do you care?"

"And when you came back, was he still gone to the bathroom?"

"No. He was sitting down. Said Cassidy and his guys had left. Then your partner came in, remember?"

"Just getting the timeline straight. When did you call in the car theft?"

"Adriano did that. Your guy was already there. No, wait, he came just after the call. Hell, I can't remember. Ask him. Ask Adriano. My head hurts. My hip hurts worse, and I'm tired. I'm going to sleep."

"Nitey-night, Doodles. I'll be around when you wake up."

"Ugh."

As Stumpf left the room, Pullman's lawyer started in. Stumpf stopped him. "He's taking a nap, counselor," the detective said. "Want to talk with me a little while he's sleeping?"

"*He's* paying my hourly, officer."

"Detective."

"Detective. Anyway, you aren't. That talk will have to wait."

"Later, then."

"Later." They left Pullman's room and headed in separate directions.

* * *

Plessy and Redding were developing their strategy. "We're target rich, Jerry," the ADA said, "and victim-rich, too. The trick is to make sure nobody slithers out. We have everybody in custody now, and the cases against Loco and Loverne won't come to trial. They'll plead, testify. We have to make sure we get Ippolito and especially Pullman."

"I'm not here to do your job, Jacob, but isn't conspiracy to commit murder, being an accomplice either before or after the fact, and all the lying – can't you make a case out of that?"

"That's how we'll go. We don't have either one of those worms' doing any personal, hands-on killing. To answer your question, yes. We can get life on all of it."

"Death penalty?"

"Not worth trying. And if we charge them with murder, they might confuse a jury enough to let them walk. There's no doubt about the conspiracy, on either one of them."

"Do they know you won't try for death?"

"No. Are you saying you can still get them to testify against each other?"

"Maybe. But Fred just told me Pullman lied to him. Pullman said Ippolito must have gone to the bathroom – some other bathroom than the one he was in – and that he was still in the front room when he left, and there before he got back, and all he did was pee."

"Wait a minute – Pullman peed, and Ippolito left after him and was back before, and went to a farther bathroom?"

"Yeah. And Ippolito told us he used the same bathroom that Pullman did, besides. And guess what? Ippolito took a dump."

"Well, that lawyer is some kind of champion crapper, then, isn't he?"

"Just one more damn thing that doesn't add up."

"Thanks for that." He folded up his notes and stood up. "We've got 'em," he said. "Got 'em both."

"Hope so. See you in court?"

Fist bump and out.

Epilogue

At their trials, Loco and Loverne pleaded guilty
to conspiracy to commit the murder of Jean
Leitner, and were given twenty-year sentences.
They received life sentences, with possibility
for parole, for the murder of Barry Cassidy. The
lesser charges were dropped.

Adriano Ippolito was convicted of conspiracy
to commit murder in the cases of both Jean
Leitner and Barry Cassidy, and as an accessory
after the fact in both murders. His lesser
charges, including making a false police report
about the theft of his car and false testimony
to detectives, also resulted in guilty verdicts.
The judge gave the maximum sentences in all
the convictions, and had them run sequentially,
for a total of over three hundred years.
Fifty-two-year-old Adriano Ippolito would
first be eligible for parole in eighty-nine years.

At Chip Pullman's trial, he faced the testi-
monies of the other three, pizza evidence, beer
bottles, telephone records, the testimony of
Ronnie McGowan, bank records, and the cat
hairs from all over Barry Cassidy's blanket,
hairs that came from his wife's cat.

Pullman got three life sentences, one for
complicity in the murder of Barry Cassidy,
another two for conspiracy in the deaths of
David and Jean Leitner. All lesser charges

were dropped. He realized that without the cat hairs, the police might still be looking for a suspect in the Leitners' deaths. And without them, Cassidy would still be alive, cheating him.

Ronnie and Carlene bought a car and moved in together. They started a Private Investigations business after "hiring" Charlie with a $15,000 signing bonus. They eventually got licensed and the three of them worked together at a legitimate version of Cassidy's collection business.

Everyone else went back to work.

Clarence "Chip" Pullman, after four years of appeals, went to the state's supermax prison, where a fellow inmate put a sharpened stick through his throat.

His recovery was slow, and when he was discharged from the prison's hospital, the guards said he got dizzy while walking back to his solitary cell. He fell and whacked his head, hard.

He lay unconscious for two days. Vanessa didn't visit him, but he woke briefly and said some incoherent things. Only one sentence was intelligible. The orderly in the room said his last words were, "I hate that damn cat."

And then he closed his eyes, his mouth, and his soul forever.

#

About Tim Kern

The author is best known as an aviation writer, with bylined features in over fifty aviation publications worldwide.

Unlike his usual fare, however, this book contains no verifiable facts, and the people and their quotes are all made up.

Kern taught economics for fifteen years, to students from high school through postgraduate levels. His nine-year radio show, *Tim Kern, Talking Sense*, aired on over 200 stations.

He has raced motorcycles and still rides regularly; he's a former car racer and race instructor, and he was a professional mechanic on a championship-winning Can-Am team. He holds a Private Pilot certificate.

Although he has other published titles, including his first book, <u>The Executive Primer</u> (serialized over three years in *SUCCESS Magazine*) and a novella best forgotten but which may yet turn into some kind of cult classic, this is his first novel.

Connect with Tim Kern

If you enjoyed this book, please take the time to write a review, and by all means, tell others (and naturally if you didn't, don't).

There are a few ways to stay in touch with the author. His Facebook page, Writings of Tim Kern, is one such method. [https://www.facebook.com/TimKernWritings/]

Direct email is another. See below.
Tim is available for speaking engagements and book signings.
And at the risk of sounding redundant, to get on Tim Kern's email list (and receive periodic free short stories and articles, questions, and advance notice of upcoming publications), send an email request to
info@timkern.com